THE CATTLEMAN'S BIG HEART

MOUNTAIN MEN OF MONTANA, BOOK 4

DANA ALDEN

ISBN 979-8-9863610-3-1

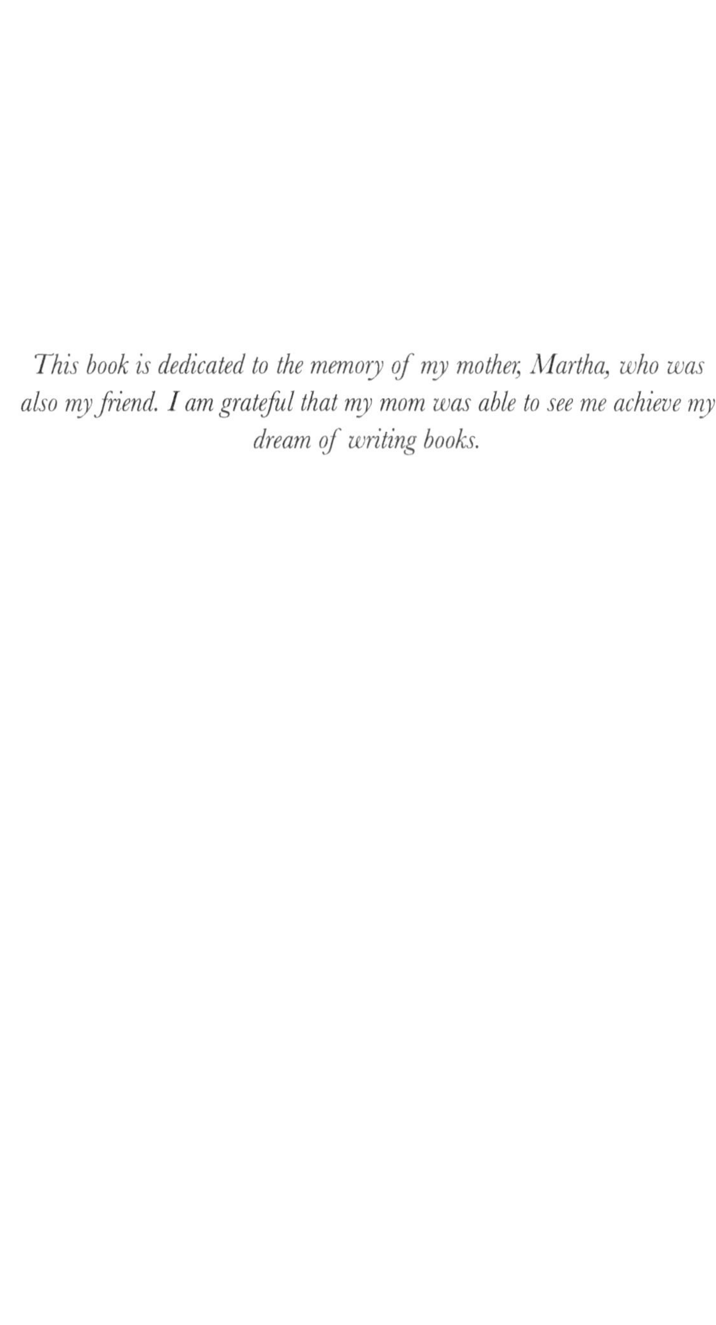

This book is dedicated to the memory of my mother, Martha, who was also my friend. I am grateful that my mom was able to see me achieve my dream of writing books.

"Pardon me, Mrs. Banks?"

Bertha looked up from her desk to see a terribly handsome man, hat in hand, filling the doorway to her parlor. He had broad shoulders and a shock of blond hair that stuck out in every direction.

He must have noticed the direction of her eyes because he added, "It's windy today."

She nodded and said, "Everyone calls me Big Bertha." She pressed the cap onto the

inkwell and stood up, closing and locking her desk. "I'm afraid we don't open until later." She looked him up and down again. "But you can come back." She sashayed across the room toward him.

His eyes widened in alarm, and his weather-beaten skin reddened. "I'm not here—that's not why—" He took a deep breath. "Ma'am."

Bertha paused. Plenty of men had come to her brothel

hoping to spend time with one of her girls. Over the years, a few had panicked and denied that was why they had come. Some young ones just ran away.

But this man was standing his ground.

"Ma'am, I came for you."

Bertha couldn't help the smile that stretched across her face. "I'm afraid I don't meet with the gentlemen anymore. But I am flattered."

She laid her hand across her décolleté as she spoke. His eyes shot from there to the ceiling. He was so clearly uncomfortable that Bertha wanted to laugh. She turned to draw back the curtain on the window to let in more light.

"No disrespect, ma'am, but that's not what I meant."

She spun around and sat on the settee, letting her skirts flutter down around her. She held out her hand to indicate the seat. "Come sit and tell me why you are here, Mr. Henry Alsobrook."

He drew back for a moment, his eyebrows raised.

"You know who I am?" he asked.

"Yes, Mr. Alsobrook. I did my research."

Alsobrook didn't speak but continued to stand in the doorway.

Bertha watched him. She could almost imagine the gears turning in his mind. She had something he needed, but he didn't want to get it from her. And he could give her something she needed, but most men wouldn't get involved with a woman like her.

Well, she could wait too. She didn't care that he wasn't a customer, but if he couldn't bring himself to sit beside her then this wasn't going to work. She looked him over again. He'd polished his boots and worn a necktie to meet her. She rather hoped he would go through with it. The discussion, at the very least.

Alsobrook was looking over the room, apparently noting

the fineness of the furniture, the fabric of the drapes and settee, and even the quality of her dress. On the walls hung prints of beautiful women, tasteful but seductive. She'd hung pictures like a saloon, originally, manly pictures of professional boxers, hunting prints, and scenic mountains. But it had encouraged the men to behave too wildly. The more feminine atmosphere reminded men they were not where they belonged and, in fact, were lucky to be there and so they had better behave.

Alsobrook finally looked back at Bertha and nodded. He stepped into the room, closing the door behind him. He hung his hat on a hook and joined her on the settee. His broad shoulders closed the space between them on the small piece of furniture.

"Ma'am—" he began.

"Mr. Alsobrook, I insist that you call me Bertha. Would you like a drink?"

"No, thank you, Mrs. Banks."

Bertha arched her eyebrows. Alsobrook straightened and started again.

"No, thank you, Miss Bertha." He pulled a folded paper from his coat pocket. "Since you know why I'm here, maybe you'd like to look at the contract."

She shook her head. "Not yet. I want to know why I should trust you with my money." He returned the paper to his pocket.

This was the sticking point for her. She had money to invest. She wanted to invest it like Cornelius Vanderbilt, whom she had read about numerous times in the papers. She wanted to become a businesswoman. An independent woman. A woman who was respected. A woman who didn't own a brothel. She wanted to sit behind the desk and let the money roll in.

Mining was hit or miss, emphasis on the miss. No one

would accept a woman banker, even if she had the capital for it. She'd been around saloons enough to know that was the life she wanted to leave behind. As for other business ventures… well, not many men wanted to go into business with a woman, especially a woman with her history. She had a few investments around town, but they were small potatoes.

She looked at the handsome man sitting beside her. He had the weathered look of a man who spent most of his time outdoors. His tanned skin made his green eyes stand out brighter.

"I am a cattleman. I grew up, back in the States, raising cows with my pa. I've done some butchering and some milking. I know my cattle. And I know this territory needs cattle. A lot of it. There's a big opportunity here." His face lit up, and he talked faster as they turned the conversation to something he was clearly comfortable with. "Not just for a few cows, but hundreds and thousands of them. The camps are growing into towns and cities, and they're not going to stop. Folks need to eat. Simple as that."

He leaned back, resting his hands on his knees.

Bertha nodded. She agreed with him. That wasn't the problem.

"Do you really think you can get the cattle up here from Texas in time? I'm told it's a little late in the season to be starting out."

Alsobrook looked Bertha in the eye. "Yes, ma'am. It'll be a push. On the one hand, the cattle have had more time to fatten up on the summer grass. On the other, early snows could trap us along the way."

"Us?"

"I'll hire some men down there. There's a fellow, my friend Nathan, already in Texas, scouting out the cattle."

"What kind are you planning on?" Bertha didn't know much about cattle, but she'd had enough men cry on her shoulder because their animals, bred for gentler climes, couldn't survive in the harsh environment of Montana Territory.

Alsobrook nodded. "I'm thinking Texas Longhorns. They're tough and can survive on the sparse rangeland we've got here."

"What about Indians?"

Alsobrook nodded again. "I'll try to avoid them, of course, but I'll also save some money to buy our way across their land if needed." He pulled out the contract for a second time, opening it and pointing. "See here? This is how much I expect to pay for the cattle, give or take. This is how much I'll need to pay the crew. This is for tolls, including the Indian kind, and other expenses that might crop up."

Bertha took the contract and studied it. "Why not take the cattle to the big meat market cities in the East?"

"Well, there's sure to be a big Indian tax going that way. And, truth is, there's a big market here."

"What's this?" Bertha pointed.

"We're going to share the profit, but instead of cash, I'm going to keep some of the cattle to build my own herd."

Bertha tapped the paper with her finger. "Now that's a good idea."

Alsobrook shook his head. "That's not part of the partnership. I've got my homestead in the Gallatin Valley, and I'll be heading out there once I sell our cattle here."

Bertha smiled. *Our* cattle. It sounded like this man was willing to do business with her. "So, it's not a problem to do business with a…woman?" She waved her arms, gesturing to the building and all that it was.

"Money's money, ma'am, and you've got a reputation as a fair player."

A knock on the front door interrupted them. Bertha excused herself to answer it. A scrawny young woman stood there, her bonneted head tipped down so Bertha couldn't see her face.

"I think you have the wrong door, my dear."

The bonnet rose briefly, offering a flash of shiny eyes. A low voice stated, "No, ma'am. I'm in the right place. My husband died in a mining accident over in Central City. I need work, and I was told to see you…that you treat your girls nicer."

Bertha glanced over her shoulder at Alsobrook. He was politely looking away, but she knew he could hear the conversation. She stepped closer to the young woman.

"Have you spoken with the pastor and his wife at the church over yonder? You might be surprised to find they can help you, especially if you're willing to consider marriage to someone you don't know so well yet."

The woman stilled like a statue. After a moment, a strangled gasp emitted from the shadows of her bonnet. A hand, red and calloused, likely from helping her husband pan for gold, reached out for a moment before she pulled away from Bertha.

"I-I—" the woman muttered, but unable to proceed, she turned and scurried down the street toward the church.

"You're welcome," Bertha called out in a cheery voice. She closed the door and turned back to Alsobrook.

He stood as she approached the couch.

"I see why so many people sing your praises," he said.

"She is not meant for this life. Some women can do it, but some…" She shrugged. "It would kill her."

Alsobrook studied her with his green eyes.

Bertha didn't want him to think she was a milksop. She flashed her best smile and gestured from her shoulders to her hips, which she then twitched, sending a wave of ruffles dancing. "Not every woman is as strong as this one."

"Yes." Alsobrook nodded, his cheeks reddening slightly.

"Quite a reputation." He glanced around, clearly looking to be saved from embarrassment, before picking up on their earlier conversation. "What about you? You're investing with a fellow you don't know."

Bertha smiled, letting one side of her mouth curve up as she tilted her head. "I can read a man fairly well. And I've looked into you." His eyes narrowed slightly as she continued. "I know you came out here and panned for gold for a bit. That you sent some money home. That you worked for the butcher shop and were reliable and trustworthy. That you don't have gambling debts. That you filed a claim for a homestead, which means you plan to stay."

She paused a moment, straightened, and dropped her smile. "I know my signature doesn't mean a hill of beans to a lot of men, but I'm a woman of my word. I expect you to be a man of yours. And if you're not…well, I know where to find you, Mr. Alsobrook." She let the gentle threat hang in the air.

His eyes widened in surprise, and then he smiled broadly. "That's fair enough, Miss Bertha, and you should call me Henry." He held out his hand.

She put her hand in his, which was warm and calloused. He didn't caress hers or ogle her or wink at her. It was her turn to be surprised. He was treating her like a business partner. She smiled back.

Bertha stood and returned to her desk. She unlocked and lowered the writing shelf. She put out a pen and inkwell and then gestured to Henry. He laid out the contracts, one copy for each of them. She signed both with a flourish.

As Henry went to sign, he read her signature aloud. "Bertha Beulah Banks."

She handed him a blotting cloth. "I was called Beebee when I was a little girl. I was always buzzing around, getting into trouble."

Back then, life had seemed so simple. Maybe she was

finally heading back in that direction. She looked at Henry and caught the merest flicker of…something in his eyes. He wasn't as immune to her as he pretended, she realized. She walked him across the room, taking his hat from the hook and passing it to him.

"Are you planning to become a rancher, then?"

"I sure hope so," Alsobrook said, that excited tone coming into his voice again. "I've got my land running up into the foothills of the mountains, outside of Bozeman. Beautiful views of the mountains and lots of good hunting. Got a nice little cabin built. Just need to add a family."

He paused, and Bertha suspected he wasn't used to sharing much about himself.

"What are your plans, Miss Bertha?"

Bertha gazed around the room. "I'm ready for something different." She said it in an offhand manner, because she couldn't bear for him, for anyone, to know how desperate she was to leave the brothel behind her. She'd worked so hard, always with her goal in mind. And now, she was betting everything on this man. He was the key to a different and better life.

They shook hands as they said goodbye. Bertha was surprised again, this time by a spark that jumped between their fingers as they touched. This was going to be an interesting partnership.

CHAPTER 2

TEXAS

"Boss, are you still sick?"

Henry groaned. He felt sicker than he'd ever felt in his life. He was sweating and shivering from chills at the same time. His throat throbbed, and his head felt like a longhorn bull was kicking him over and over.

"Need a day," he struggled to say. "Find some range for the cattle. Water."

"I know they need water," Nathan said, with all the exasperation of an old cowhand.

"Me. Water for me." Henry's voice was failing.

"Oh. Right, boss." Nathan grabbed the canteen and held it to Henry's lips. Henry struggled to swallow. "You're burning up. I'll see if there's a doc in town. Take 'er easy, boss."

Henry fell back on the bedroll, eyes closed, and listened to Nathan mount his horse and trot off. He could do nothing but wait there, prostrate with illness, out in the open, surrounded by rocks and grass and not much else. He struggled to open his eyes. In the distance, he could see the dust rising in the air from the hundreds of cattle he had bought only days ago. The folks in the little town wouldn't be happy if he kept his herd nearby, eating up the rangeland. He wasn't a local, and they didn't owe him anything.

No one in the state of Texas cared a bit about him, truth be told, except his buddy Nathan. No one else even knew him. There was no family nearby to remember him or grieve for him. No wife. No sons or daughters. He wondered whether his mother—if she was still alive—would care to know if he died. She'd left his pop and him so many years ago, he figured she likely wouldn't care. Certainly, his father and stepmother wouldn't be broken up about it.

Above him, the wispy clouds drifted north. It was so quiet he could hear the rustle of something small in the dry grass. He hoped it was a mouse rather than a snake. Either way, he found himself too weak to care.

They were supposed to be heading north already, to Montana Territory. Henry couldn't figure out the date, but he knew he should be concerned about snow. The sun was rising, and it would be a hot day for him and the cattle. Why was he worried about snow? All he knew was that he had a small crew —it was all he could afford—and, except for Nathan, he didn't trust the men to get there safely without him.

Henry pulled the blanket up around his shoulders and looked up at the blue sky striped with hints of clouds. *All he could afford*. He wasn't sure he dared to pay a doctor. He had kept just enough money to buy a few supplies along the trip north and bribe local Indians to be allowed to cross their land. If this trip failed, he'd be left with nothing.

Less than nothing because he had invested in the cattle with a partner. He'd owe money. And his land—he had to get moving soon. He had a home—an *empty* home. A despairing conviction tormented him. *I'm never going to get ahead—*

The thoughts swirled around his confused mind. Henry

tried to straighten them out, but a dark weight smothered him from the inside out. He drifted uneasily.

"Boss?" Nathan gently shook Henry. "I've brought the doc."

Henry forced his lids open. The sun was high in the sky, but Nathan was holding his hat between the sun and Henry, shadowing his eyes.

A man with big muttonchops and a leather vest crouched down beside Henry.

"He's got the rash," the man said. He put his hand on Henry's forehead. Then, he pulled Henry's jaw open and looked inside his mouth.

"Are you my partner?" Henry asked.

Nathan and the doc glanced at each other.

"I'm the doctor here. The sawbones and the barber too," the man said as he held Henry's wrist to check his pulse. "You must mean Nathan here."

"No…no…" Henry muttered. "The one in…in…" He couldn't remember. He snatched his hand away from the doc. Why was this man touching him? "B...B..."

"Don't get frustrated, Henry," the doc said. "It's just a name. Tell me about this fellow."

"Gave me money. Investment. Bring the cattle to the miners."

"So, your partner had the money. Is he a miner? Did he strike it rich?"

Henry had to think about it. Images of different people swirled through his mind, but he couldn't identify them. "I don't think so. He has a business…but…"

He wanted to pound the ground at his side, but all that happened was his hand flopped off the blanket. He groaned once more and let his eyes shut.

He listened to the doctor. "Your boss ain't going anywhere for a week or more. He's got the scarlet fever, and if he survives, it'll be because of God's good grace or that the Devil simply don't want him. I'm just hoping we don't see an outbreak like in '58."

There was a pause, and Henry thought the men must be as surprised as he was to feel the earth spinning beneath them.

"You got a place to nurse him, Doc? He can't lie here, and I got to tend the cattle."

"Tie him to his horse and follow me. I've got a room."

Someone was singing…a frog was singing, "B.B.….B.B.….B.B.…Banks! B.B. Banks!" Henry opened his eyes. He looked at Nathan. "Who is B.B. Banks?"

Nathan shrugged before he grabbed Henry's arms to haul him to his feet. "Your partner? Is that the fellow who invested with you?"

An image flashed before Henry's eyes. A knock-you-off-your-feet beautiful woman with blond curls piled on her head, soft-looking skin and gray-blue eyes, rounded shoulders and ruby lips. He knew, somehow, that he would feel better if he was with this woman.

"Prettiest fellow I ever saw," he mumbled as he collapsed into Nathan, and everything went black.

CHAPTER 3

Smoke filled the air along with the crackling sound of burning wood. Bertha scrambled to shove an armload of dresses out the window. The building wasn't going to survive. She knew that already. But she and her girls needed the dresses and shoes. She grabbed armloads and tossed them out. She could barely hear them bouncing along the porch roof because of the shouts of the men outside. Women's shoes and boots… not easy to come by in Montana Territory.

Bertha bent over as a wracking cough consumed her. She dropped to her knees to pull her strongbox from under the bed. There wasn't much in there. She pulled a gold dust poke from the box. The red wax seal was already broken, and there wasn't much gold dust left in it. *Dammit, where was Alsobrook?* She shoved it into her pocket. A few pieces of gold jewelry. One pendant with a blue sapphire. She shoved those into another pocket. And a photograph. She slid it into her bodice.

"Bertha!" Someone was coming up the stairs. "Bertha!"

She left the box open on the floor and used the bed to

brace herself as she stood up. Smoke swirled around her head, and she took one final look around the room. There was nothing else she could carry out. The girls had escaped already. She'd seen to that. And she'd seen Kit outside, gathering the things she'd been tossing out the window.

The door burst open, and a wall of smoke and heat flashed into the room. It was Reg, her friend and the owner of a mercantile down the street.

"Always rescuing people, aren't you, Reg?" Bertha asked. Her smoke-damaged voice belied the cool comment.

"Only lovely ladies," he said as he shoved the door closed behind him. "We're going out the window." He walked in a crouch, trying to keep his head out of the thick smoke hugging the ceiling. Bertha already had one leg over the windowsill when he reached her. He held her arms as she slid her other leg out and wiggled out feetfirst with her stomach on the sill. He held her until her feet reached the porch roof.

A loud cracking, crashing sound burst from the inside of the building, and the whole structure lurched sideways. Bertha pulled her hands free and dropped to her knees.

"Hurry up, Reg!" a voice shouted.

Bertha looked through her watering eyes.

Another friend, J.B., was leaning over the porch roof, holding his hand out to Bertha. "This way, Bertha!"

She reached him just as another wracking cough consumed her. Her eyes screwed shut, and she couldn't do anything but collapse. She felt J.B.'s arms drag her off the porch.

"Hold the ladder," he shouted, and suddenly they were lurching down, and other arms grabbed her and pulled her away from the building.

The cool night air hit her, and she began to shiver and gasp.

"Reg?" she croaked.

"He's out," said J.B. as he rushed off to join the bucket brigade.

Bertha was tucked into a scratchy wool blanket. Someone wrapped an arm around her and tried to lead her away. She pulled back and instead leaned on the hitching rail across the street to watch the inferno. Everything she'd worked for all these years was burning.

"Damn smoke…" she muttered as she wiped her eyes, trying to clear the blur of men running around.

With her sight cleared, what she saw horrified her. This wasn't just a disorganized bucket brigade. Instead, there appeared to be at least two groups of men, one hauling their leather fire buckets toward her building, and the other toward the lawyer's office next door. The lawyer himself was running from man to man, shouting offers of compensation if the men would save his building instead of the brothel.

He made a mistake when he grabbed the handle of the bucket held by Harald, trying to drag it and the young man toward his office. Harald was enamored with Lily, one of Bertha's girls. Harald yanked the bucket back and pulled the lawyer straight into his other fist at the same time.

One of the men hauling for the lawyer dropped his bucket and leapt onto Harald's back. From there, it became an all-out melee, men using the thick leather buckets to whale on each other, fists flying. One man threw his painted wooden fire bucket to the side as he dove into the brawl. The bucket landed in the fire, sizzling and then flickering yellow as it rolled away.

Bertha's hands rose to cover her mouth as she watched the flaming bucket. What little chance there was of saving her building was gone. Her heart was breaking. She had struggled so hard, and in the worst ways, to get to the point where she could build her own building. A refuge for herself and the young women who worked for her. She made sure they were safe and taken care of. Maybe it wasn't what any of them wanted to be doing, but sometimes there wasn't a choice. There wasn't a choice for Bertha, back when it started, but she'd thought she was going to leave this life behind, finally. She'd been mere months away from starting fresh somewhere new, as a respectable widow, where no one knew her history.

She clenched her eyes and her fists tightly. She felt her fingernails digging into the palms of her hands. The shouts of the men and the crackle of the fire slowly faded. She could do this. She'd gotten through worse situations.

The tightness in her chest slowly loosened. Bertha opened her eyes and adjusted the blanket again. The brawl continued, but Bertha ignored it. She pulled herself away from the railing and looked around.

Kit had borrowed a wagon and parked it down the street. Among the ruffles and lace sat her girls: Lily, Mary, Eugenie, and Betty. Mary and Lily were weeping, their tears reflecting the orange glow of the fire. What would happen to them? Eugenie looked as though she were about to be ill. And perhaps she might be. Smoke inhalation could do that to you, but truth was Eugenie was in the family way. She'd only told Bertha last week. And Betty…poor Betty. She was still recovering from a beating she'd received from a scary patron three days ago. Though Bertha had rushed upstairs the moment she'd heard the screams, gun in hand, she hadn't been quick enough to prevent a black eye, a loose tooth, and bruises all over Betty's face and neck. Now, the girl looked simply stunned. At least that fellow was walking with a limp from the bullet she put in his tail end.

Bertha took a deep breath. It was a mistake. She doubled over. She coughed so hard, it felt like her eyelids were turning inside out. She felt a gentle hand on her back. When she finally could stand upright, she saw that it was Reg's wife, Josie.

"Come, Bertha. Reg and J.B. and some others are still trying to put out the fire, but there's nothing you can do. Let's see if the hotel will have room for you and the girls. If not, we'll make room in the merc for the night."

'Have room for'…that was a bit of code for 'will allow,' thought Bertha. They'd allowed Josie's acting troupe to stay there that past spring, so perhaps…Virginia City wasn't too high in the instep yet.

She straightened her shoulders and arranged the blanket like it was a fine shawl.

"Thank you, Josie."

She took one last look at the burning brothel. This wasn't how she planned to end her career as a madam, but it looked like she didn't have a choice. She and Josie worked their way over to the wagon, dodging buckets and bystanders. Several men tipped their hats to her, but it was their pitying looks that stuck in her craw. She nodded regally, thanking the men still trying to put out the fire, but otherwise didn't look back.

"Bertha! Bertha!" Lily cried. "You're alive!"

"What are we going to do?"

"Oh, Bertha! I'm scared!"

"I am alive," Bertha said. "And so are you. Kit, I'm glad you're safe too. I don't plan to spend a single night on the street, and neither shall you. Take us to the hotel, Kit." Bertha and Josie climbed up into the wagon. Josie sat beside Eugenie and took her hand. Bertha sat between Lily and Mary. She opened her arms, and the girls tucked themselves in, nestling their heads into her neck like little children. "There, there, girls. Don't be sappy. You'll be alright. I promise."

A flare of light and shouts of men drew her attention. The roof to the brothel collapsed in.

Bertha tipped her head back and closed her eyes for a moment. When she opened them, she saw that the smoke obscured much of the night sky above, but if she looked west, she could see thousands of stars sparkling still. A tear rolled down her cheek. It never rained when you needed it.

CHAPTER 4

TEXAS

Henry eyed the storm clouds above and shook his head. Even that small motion caused him to feel light-headed, so he grabbed the pommel of the saddle.

"Keep it steady, Nugget," he murmured to his horse. The restless animal danced beneath him.

The first time he'd seen Nugget had been at an auction. The horse had been dancing and bucking around a paddock, acting as crazy as could be.

"What a nugget," an old-timer had said.

Once Henry had realized that the horse was being stung by hornets, he'd taken a second look. And he was glad he had. The loyal animal had seen him through a lot, and it looked like a bad storm was next.

"Doesn't look good, does it?" Nathan said, looking at Henry.

Henry knew he looked a sight. He'd been sick as a horse for a week. The doc had wanted him to stay and rest longer, but there hadn't been a choice. They needed to keep the cattle moving, for grass, and also if Henry didn't get the cattle north before the winter weather hit, all would be lost. He'd struggled to stay on the horse the past few days, but so far, he was surviving. It was amazing how desperate need could fight through even the worst exhaustion. He'd worked long and hard to get to this point, and feeling lower than the belly of a snake wasn't going to stop him.

"Head round that way." Henry pointed. "And make sure those other fellas are ready for a storm. We can't have the cattle spooking and running."

Nathan nodded and loped off.

Henry surveyed the herd. Nathan had kept them moving while Henry was sick, but even a few days on the trail and they were starting to lose weight. Everything depended on getting them north. Then he could sell most of the herd to the butchers in the mining towns but keep a select few to start building his own herd. He smiled grimly as he turned his horse to keep a heifer from stepping too far from the herd.

That was what he was working toward: his own herd. He wanted to raise cattle, just like he'd done growing up. But he was late getting to Texas and later still heading back north. It would be damn cold when he finally got home. And home was a cabin only partially completed. The logs were up, and the roof was on, but he hadn't chinked the wood or finished the fireplace. He had a field of potatoes that needed harvesting too.

He shook his head again. He'd been doing that a lot on this trip.

At least he didn't have a family to worry about yet.

A gust of wind had Henry tilting in his saddle. The horse danced around, and the sky darkened. A low rumble followed by a distant flash of light brought Henry's attention back to the cattle. The animals were grazing and chewing, and then, all at once, the rain poured out of the sky.

Thunder boomed overhead, followed by a crack as lightning struck a tree on a nearby butte. The cows threw up their heads and lowed, and Henry ran his horse along them, calling out, "Whoa, whoa. It's okay, lil' critters. Don't get your knickers in a twist. Slow down. Slow down."

Maybe he could hold them. He squinted through the rain and saw Nathan doing the same, and farther to the east the other hands were doing the same, too, he hoped. And then he hoped no more.

Thunder roared overhead like a herd of bison. Lightning flashed and streaked and crackled, and that was it. The cattle stampeded.

Henry found himself in a living landslide of horns and hooves and twelve-hundred-pound bodies. He and Nugget were swept away in the torrent. Around him, he'd see an animal lose their footing and disappear like a ship sunk in an angry sea of brown. Time blurred as the storm flashed and boomed.

Suddenly, a heifer directly in his path tripped and tipped forward as one of its front hooves sank into a prairie dog burrow.

Instinctively, Henry rose into the half-seated position and clutched his horse's mane. His breathing slowed as the lightning flashed in perfect harmony with his horse's wheezing, and without thinking, Henry relaxed and let Nugget do his job and jump.

Time sped up instantly as his horse landed. Miraculously, Henry found the herd had shifted away, leaving them like driftwood on the edge of a raging river.

Finally, the thunder rolled away; the lightning flashed farther and farther in the distance. The rain lessened, and the animals calmed.

As Henry began to collect cattle, he kept looking up,

hoping to see his team. After a bit, in the distance, he saw some of the hired hands riding along the herd.

Looking back in the direction from which they had come, Henry inspected the damage. Amongst the trampled brush, injured cattle thrashed and emitted sorrowful mewling. Then Henry's eyes fell on a horse lying prone, trying in vain to right itself with two broken legs.

From his position, he couldn't see the rider, and he galloped to the aid of one of his men. As he dismounted, he saw Nathan's still body, crushed under the weight of his mare. His friend was dead. With one swift movement, Henry drew his pistol and put the mare out of her misery. Removing his hat, he turned and muttered, "I'm sorry, my friend."

He trotted out, found the other hands and told them to gather up all the cattle they could. Then he returned to Nathan's side. He scraped out a low grave to place his friend in and then collected stones to cover him. He knelt in the dirt, damp seeping into the denim at his knees, praying for God to look over Nathan's soul.

Henry dropped his head, feeling the grief merge with exhaustion. Life was awfully hard out West.

When he looked up, there were two Indians standing on a butte in the distance, watching him. Comanche? Kiowa? Henry wasn't sure. He stood up and slowly walked to his horse. He pulled out his rifle, a Remington breechloader which he knew was better than most weapons they likely had but wouldn't mean much if there were a whole party of them heading his way. He stood there, legs braced, cradling his gun, looking right at the other men. He wouldn't attack them, but he would defend his cattle—and his future—to the death. Thing was, with the doctor bill and the need to hire extra men when he got sick, he didn't have any money left to bribe the Indians to let him pass—if that was even an option.

After a few minutes, the Indians turned away. Henry

mounted his horse, tipped his hat to Nathan's grave, and trotted off toward his hired hands. Whatever cattle the men had managed to round up would have to be enough. It wasn't worth losing their lives over a few strays, even if it did bode poorly for his profits.

Instead of a night of rest, as he'd hoped for, they were going to have to travel all that night and then some. He wasn't even sure they'd be able to rest at Fort Phil Kearney when they finally got there. They might have to just keep going.

He looked at the sun in the sky, burning through the remaining clouds. There were a few more hours of sunlight, to be sure. He squeezed his legs and clucked at his horse to move on.

Henry allowed his thoughts to drift. He pictured the beautiful Bertha Beulah Banks. He imagined her pleasure when he knocked on her door and handed her a couple of poke bags of gold nuggets and dust, the proceeds from the sale of the cattle. He imagined the softness of her skin as they shook hands, a brilliant smile on her face. Perhaps she'd lean forward and kiss his cheek, letting him smell her feminine, flowery scent. Her blond curls would brush against his face.

He knew that their whole transaction would last but a few minutes, but at this moment, cold and wet, preparing for a night of trudging at best and fighting at worst, she was the beacon that kept him moving forward. That, and knowing he'd be set and ready to work his own land with his own crops and own cattle. No more working for another man. No more scrabbling in the dirt, hoping there might be a speck of gold dust there. A living not based on luck but on hard work. That he could do.

And maybe someday, there'd be a woman as pretty as Big Bertha waiting for him at the door of his cabin.

CHAPTER 5

It was a beautiful fall day. The sky was bright blue with puffy clouds floating by. A light breeze kicked up, bringing the pungent smell of burnt, wet wood to her nostrils. Bertha sat on a bench on the boardwalk across from what had been everything to her. Her home, her livelihood.

She watched as miners and merchants, farmers and gamblers all paused to look at the shell of charred timbers. The saloon on one side and the lawyer's office on the other had some charring, but very little, considering the condition of her property. The saloon keeper was already out there, replacing boards and logs. Amusingly enough, he was selling drinks through the opened-up wall until he finished the repairs.

"Big Bertha, luv, I came straightaway when I heard this morning."

Bertha looked up to see Gimpy Pete. The man, freckled so heavily he looked brown, had a terrible limp from his injuries in the War Between the States. He'd been working over in Hungry Hollow, panning and placing for gold.

"Hello, Pete. I don't suppose you've come to pay back my investment?" Bertha drawled. She smiled gently, knowing the answer in advance.

"'Fraid not. I can give you this, though." Pete held up a small poke bag which Bertha guessed was worth about twenty dollars in gold dust. "That's all I got right now."

She looked at his frayed cuffs and the pants held up by a belt that hadn't any more holes for tightening.

"You keep it," she said, injecting a light note in her voice. "I know you'll hit it big soon, and then you can give me what you promised. Until then, you've got a family to prepare for."

Relief dropped Pete's shoulders. He tipped his hat. "You're ace-high, Big Bertha."

Bertha watched him limp away. Twenty dollars wouldn't make so much difference for her at this point, but it would for him. His wife and boys were due to arrive on the stage from Salt Lake City any day now. Once he had their help and support, she knew he'd find every speck of gold on his claim or die trying. She could be patient, like a Vanderbilt waiting for his train tracks to be laid. She'd wait to be paid back with the annual 2.5 percent interest next spring.

She turned her attention back to the smoldering ruins. She didn't know if her building could have been saved, but the division of the bucket brigades and the brawl had likely been the tipping point.

She'd planned to sell the building when she closed shop. That had been part of her plan. One more gold nugget for her new life. She'd come to Virginia City early on, chosen a prime location and opened her brothel, always knowing she would sell it one day.

Lily and Mary had come with her from the California gold fields. Other girls had come and gone since then. Girls who, like Bertha all those years ago, found themselves doing something they never thought they'd do. The difference was, Bertha thought vehemently, they'd had her—Bertha—to look out for them. To protect them.

But lately, that hadn't been the case. Eugenie was with child; Betty had been beaten up, and they were all homeless. Lily might be all right. Her favorite caller, Harald, had come to the hotel early this morning, terribly concerned that she had been hurt. Bertha had turned away when he had fallen to his knees next to Lily's bed, grabbing her hand between his and pressing it to his cheek. The hotelier had stood there, sputtering, because Harald had pushed past him and up the stairs, calling Lily's name until Bertha had opened the door. Bertha pushed the hotelier out of the room and closed the door behind her. With any luck, when she returned to the hotel, she'd find that Harald had proposed, and he and Lily were ready to get married.

She would give Lily a little bit of gold to help them start their new lives together. At least, that was her plan, if there was any left.

Mary…well, she had been talking about going to the gold fields in Arizona, where the weather was warmer. She hadn't liked the long winter last year and wasn't looking forward to this one. She'd have to leave soon, before the stagecoaches shut down for the winter. Perhaps Betty would go with her.

Bertha drew her shawl closer. Delia, J.B.'s wife, had lent her this one. All of her clothes smelled of smoke and were covered with soot and dirt from throwing them out the window onto the street. Delia ran the local washateria. She'd taken most of the girls' clothes last night to start washing. Bertha imagined Delia scrubbing the clothes while her new baby boy, wrapped in a warm blanket, cooed in the bassinet beside her.

She pulled in her errant thoughts and looked around again. There'd been a couple of men interested in her building. She'd been inclined, though, to sell it to Tall Tilly, a woman of the night ready to strike out on her own. Bertha wasn't sure she'd be interested now that the building was gone. Tall Tilly was a bit of a card shark too. She could rebuild with a layout better suited to hosting cards and still have rooms upstairs for any girls she hired.

Bertha wasn't sure how they'd feel about the land itself, alone. The land was sellable, but she wouldn't make the same amount. The only person who was checking out the building presently was Reg. The sheriff had gone to Bannack and wasn't expected back for a few days. Reg was walking around, studying the charred remains. Finally, he crossed the street to Bertha.

"Looks like it started in the kitchen."

"It doesn't really matter, does it?" she asked, looking up at him.

"I suppose not." He looked at her with pity in his eyes.

Bertha stood up. "Don't worry about me, Reg. I always bounce back. I was planning to close up shop anyway. I've made some investments, and when they come in, I'll be done with this life." She pulled her shoulders back and smiled. She knew the smile didn't reach her eyes. She knew that Reg could see this too. But he went along with it.

"You're a survivor, Bertha. No question about that. You just tell Josie or me how we can help until then."

Bertha reached out a hand and placed it on Reg's wrist, squeezing gently. As he turned to walk away, she said, "You're both too good to me."

Reg nodded and kept going. "Probably so."

Laughter burst out from Bertha. It was a little scary because she could feel the hysteria on the far edge of it. And yet how good it felt to laugh.

"Now that's a sound I wasn't expecting."

Bertha turned to see Joshua Reynolds striding toward her, worry lines creasing his brow. She held out her hands, and he took them in his own, studying her face. "Bertha, I was down at the other end of the gulch when I heard the news. I came straightaway. I imagined you prostrate on a couch, weeping. I should have known better."

"Indeed, you should have, Joshua," Bertha said. She gestured to the shell across the street. "I don't even own a couch anymore." She said it lightly. It's just a couch, she told herself.

"Come with me." Joshua led her down the street and to a saloon that they'd visited many times before. Usually they sat at the window, the better to watch the comings and goings as they chatted. This time, they sat at a table away from the window, away from the sight of the burned remains and the men standing around and recounting again and again the flaming drama of the night before.

Joshua walked to the bar to get them each a whiskey. While he waited, he looked in the mirror, smoothing his muttonchop whiskers. His chestnut-brown whiskers and curly head of hair were a source of pride to him that made Bertha smile.

She was glad they had come here. She wasn't a big drinker, and certainly not in the morning, but today was unique. At least this bar had imported whiskey from the States, not the local homemade, flavored by who knows what. Last month, a couple of fellows had died from drinking bad whiskey.

The door opened, and Kit walked in with a piece of paper in hand.

"Bertha! You got a telegram."

A telegram? Bertha had never received one before. The telegraph office had opened in Virginia City only a few months back. And she didn't have anyone to send her one.

Every eye in the saloon turned her way. Joshua, standing across the room, raised his eyebrows.

She took the paper and unfolded it.

It was from Alsobrook. She'd hoped he'd be back by now.

Illness Indians Storms Delayed.

That was it.

Not even long enough to warrant a STOP.

Delayed. One week? One month? One winter?

Bertha folded the telegraph precisely and handed it back to Kit.

"Take it back to the room, Kit."

The excited light in Kit's eyes dimmed. Telegraphs were used for really good news or really bad news, and clearly Bertha didn't think it was good news. She wasn't going to explain it here though. She wasn't going look vulnerable.

Joshua sat down in the seat beside Bertha. He placed a jigger of whiskey in front of her. "What's the news? Has your ship come in?"

"My ship is still at sea." She picked up the glass and swirled its contents gently.

"Come to Bozeman."

"Pardon?"

Joshua leaned forward, a smile lighting his face. "Come to Bozeman. Leave this life behind. Start fresh."

Bertha felt something inside her ripping apart. That was what she wanted: to start fresh. She'd planned on it for years. Dreamed about it and worked toward it. But nearly all her savings were gone. She'd invested with Alsobrook and Gimpy Pete and Sally Sash, and even former slave Samuel Lincoln, whose mine in the foothills had collapsed but he was digging it out, and she was sure it was going to pay out. But not yet.

"I'm afraid it won't be that easy," she said.

"I'll help you, Bertha. I'll close off a floor of my hotel just for you."

"I-I don't need a floor, Joshua. I'm done. Done with my business."

"Of course you are. Now's your chance to be the lady you deserve to be. I'll be going back and forth between Virginia City and Bozeman until next summer. We can take the winter to get to know each other better and…plan for the future. Our future." He placed his hand on hers for a moment.

She looked at it, confused and astonished. And scared. Scared of the hope that welled inside her that always seemed to end up squashed.

She and Joshua had been friends this past year. He'd hinted at his admiration but always kept a respectful attitude. They'd talked business and alluded to hopes and dreams for the future, but never had she thought Joshua wanted more from her: a future.

She'd never thought any man would want a future with her.

"I'll take care of you until we can head back East." He lowered his voice. "Then Big Bertha will leave Virginia City. No one here will know what happened to her. The people of St. Louis will never know about her. You'll have a new name there. Your past can be erased. You can have the life you deserve. With me."

A new name? Marriage? A myriad of emotions clashed throughout Bertha. Hope and fear, sadness and gratefulness. She'd never thought any man would consider marrying her after all she had been through. For the first time in many years, since her life was first upended, she wanted to simply get up and run. Run and run until all her troubles were left behind.

Unfortunately, she knew the troubles didn't stay where you tried to leave them.

She opened her mouth to speak. Part of her head told her the obvious thing to say. "Of course!"

But part of her head wouldn't let her. Wouldn't let her give up her independence and self- determination to be a kept woman in hopes that he would marry her next year. Something inside of her was yelling, *Don't be a fool! Say yes!* But something else was whispering *Don't let yourself be fooled! You can't have that life. Not after what you've done.*

She saw the questioning in Joshua's eyes, wondering why she didn't jump at his offer. She thought of the life she had been living and people she cared for.

"My girls."

Joshua sat back, shaking his head. "You need to leave them behind. You can't start fresh with them hanging on your skirts."

She knew he was right. She couldn't take up the life of a lady with the sullied young women hanging on. But she wasn't ready to leave them behind. She had to launch them from her nest as best she could. Her thoughts scrambled. If only Alsobrook returned and her investment paid out. She'd have the money to set each girl safely on her own feet and enough to safeguard herself from this plan failing.

And then she remembered: Alsobrook wasn't home, and his nice little cabin was sitting empty. It was his delay that left her in this position. It was the least he could do. Meanwhile, she would sell her land here in Virginia City. That would give her the money to help settle the girls and to buy winter supplies and pay for transportation to the cabin. She smiled, feeling in control again.

"I will come to the Gallatin Valley, Joshua, near to Bozeman. But I know where I'm going to stay, at least at first, and I'll have my girls with me until I can get them settled."

Joshua's eyes blazed. He raised his glass. "To our future."

Bertha raised her glass and clinked it with Joshua's.

CHAPTER 6

The brisk wind ruffled the fields of golden grasses. The skies above were bluebird blue, and the sun on Henry's face gave him the last push he needed. He was nearly home. The Gallatin Valley had never looked so good. There wasn't much green left, except along the creeks, but there was a lot of forage in the valley for the cattle. Henry wished he could take the animals straight to Virginia City, but both he and the cattle needed a break. The cattle would benefit from some plumping up, but Henry—he wouldn't make it. After Nathan had died, after another hand had bugged out when they ran into some Crow Indians, well, Henry had never recovered from his illness in Texas.

He leaned onto the neck of his horse. The horse knew where it was and seemed to be herding the cows there without interference from Henry. When he got to the creek at the foothills, he left the animals to graze. They would be happy not to be on the move again. He waved to the men still working the cattle. They were exhausted too.

The horse picked up its gait as they approached the homestead. Through his grit-crusted eyes, Henry saw a woman pulling potatoes from his field. She wore a plain dress, though in rather a bright blue—like the sky—with a sun hat on her head. Another woman stood beside her, holding her apron out to collect the potatoes. It was so much like his dreams, he wondered if he really did have a family. A wife and daughter?

He wanted to push himself up to sitting, but he simply couldn't. After a brief moment of confusion, when he wondered if he were in the right place, he'd felt an anger rise up in him. This was the right place. His place. And someone had moved in and was harvesting his vegetables, and dammit, he'd fight for his land.

The women looked up. The woman in blue raised her hand to tip her hat to allow her to see more clearly. Then she began running, leaving the other behind.

"Oh, Henry!"

Henry? She knew him?

He rode up to the cabin door. There was a water bucket sitting on one side of the doorway and a broom leaning against the wall on the other. He slid off the horse, desperately hanging onto the saddle so he didn't tip right over.

"I was afraid you'd never get back." Then, after a long pause, the woman continued. "You look terrible. Let me help you."

She stepped up next to him and tucked herself under his shoulder then slid her arm around his waist. She was treating him like she knew him, like they were close. His eyelids were drooping, and he just wanted to sleep, even while an angry leprechaun danced around inside him.

He looked at the woman half dragging him toward the cabin door. She wore a sky-blue dress of a finer fabric than most homesteaders wore. He could see tiny holes in the fabric where there had probably been ruffles and lace sewn on, in a different life. The woman was curvy. Very curvy. And strong. She had a blond braid hanging over her shoulder. She tipped her head up to look at him.

Henry stopped in his tracks. "Big Bertha?"

That brilliant smile flashed across her face.

"The one and only." She laughed, gently tugging him forward again, toward the doorway.

"What—?"

"There's lots to tell you, Henry. But it looks like you need rest first." She sniffed. "And a bath."

Henry halted on the threshold.

"Now wait a gosh-darn minute. What's going on here? This is my property—"

As his eyes adjusted to the dim light inside the cabin, he saw a rug on the dirt floor, a table with four chairs around it, new shelves on the walls, even a curtain in the doorway to the bedroom. Even the back wall had been chinked and daubed—*though not as smoothly as I'd have done it myself*, the errant thought floated through his mind.

Bertha had moved in.

Into his cabin.

He felt a wildfire raging inside of him. He wasn't aware of the woman at his side physically. He felt like he was looking down on the man and woman standing in the threshold of the small cabin. It wasn't him. It couldn't be him. He'd worked so hard to get there. He'd almost died.

The curtain parted, and a third woman peeked out.

Three women. He tried to speak, and all he could do was choke.

"Henry, you're weaker than a kitten, skinny as a fence post, and you smell like the cattle you've been traveling with. Come sit, and we'll talk after you're rested," said Bertha as she led him to a chair. "Eugenie, pass me the special stuff."

The young woman, Eugenie, slid out from behind the

curtain, tucking a wrap around her shoulders. She was very thin, except for a small belly. *There was a woman with child in his home.* And she wasn't *his* woman, and it wasn't *his* child.

He collapsed into the chair, gripping the sides of the table to stay upright. Everything he'd done was leading toward a home with a family to be proud of. This wasn't right. He had to get rid of them. How could he bring a wife back here with this crowd? He didn't understand, and his head was fuzzy.

Big Bertha slid a cup of whiskey in front of him. He drank half of it, placed it on the table and closed his eyes for a moment. Finally, he looked at the woman sitting across from him, looking so different from the fancified woman he'd met in Virginia City. She looked like a hardworking pioneer woman.

She was as beautiful as he remembered, though.

But this wasn't how they were supposed to meet again.

"What are you doing here?" He could hear the harshness of his voice, but he didn't have it in him for feminine civilities right then.

Bertha assessed him. "I'll put my cards on the table, Henry. My building burned down. I lost most of my possessions. My other investments aren't ready to pay out. All I've got left is tied up in that cattle. I don't have a tail feather left. I have nowhere to live and no money to go there until you pay out the profits." She shrugged.

Henry stilled. He'd lost time and pounds of flesh on the trip. He wasn't sure how much profit he had to give her. He tried to remember how many head of cattle were left, tried to calculate. The whiskey in his ravaged body was hitting him hard. He tried to shake it off.

Bertha's eyes widened.

"There will be profits, won't there be?" She gripped her hands together so hard her knuckles turned white. At the same time, her beautiful face turned red.

Henry shrugged, not caring anymore. He was just so tired.

He took his glass of whiskey and shot back the remainder. He closed his eyes as he savored it.

Henry was in bed. He must have fallen asleep, but he didn't know how he'd gotten into bed. It was so much more comfortable than a bedroll on the ground. It was also bigger than the one he'd built. He sat up, leaning back on his elbows, and looked around. His bed was tucked between the foot of another smaller bed and the north wall. Dresses hung from pegs on the wall, some with frills and fripperies. He wished they'd added the pegs in an even, straight line.

How had he gotten saddled with these females? How could he get them out? He wasn't sure he could pay Bertha back without selling all the cattle, and then his hopes for next year and beyond were crushed. He could scrape together a living on his homestead, but he wanted to prosper. That was why a man came west: for a chance to make it rich on his own.

Henry rubbed his hand over his face.

He'd been shaved.

He ran his fingers through his hair. It was clean and brushed. He lifted the covers and saw he was naked and pretty darn clean for a man who'd been on the trail for a month.

He, Henry Alsobrook, had been stripped naked, bathed, and put to bed by the most glorious madam in Virginia City, if not the whole of Montana Territory. And he didn't remember it.

He dropped his head back on the pillow. He had a whole lot of things to figure out and cattle to take care of, but right now he could only think about how it was a crying shame that he didn't remember.

CHAPTER 7

Bertha pulled on the reins of her horse, aiming to guide a young steer back to the herd. The cowboys made it look so easy. But those huge horns that spread out from the animal's head, six feet across, made her and her horse skittish. How they'd traveled thousands of miles without stabbing each other or getting caught up in brush and branches, she didn't know.

She surveyed the herd. The cattle were skinnier than she'd like but otherwise seemed healthy enough. She'd been watching and waiting for weeks for Henry to bring the herd in. She wanted to wrap them in woolen flannel and tuck them safely in a box. She felt her insides fighting again, between hope—now that the herd was here—and anger that her future depended on this scrawny batch of cows.

The gelding turned his head to look east. Bertha followed with her own eyes to see Henry arriving on horseback.

"You're awake," she said.

Henry was terribly skinny, the tendons in his neck sticking out. He was nothing but a mass of ropy muscle, all of him. She knew from bathing him the day before. Dark circles shadowed his eyes. He was still a handsome man but one at the end of his rope. Well, he wasn't the only one.

"Yes, ma'am." He glanced at her, but his attention returned to the cattle. In the distance, he watched a couple of young men working the cattle, pushing the wanderers back into the herd. He gritted his teeth.

"Who's that?" he growled.

"Young Kit over there," Bertha said as she pointed toward the Bridger Mountains. "And Charlie over yonder to the west. I had to send to town for him."

Henry looked at her. "Why did you replace my men?"

Anger won out at this point. Bertha looked Henry straight in the eyes. "Because *our* investment needed tending, and *you* were out cold, and *your* hands demanded payment and to be on their way. *I* paid them, based on *our* contract that *you* wrote up, and sent them off to get stinking drunk in town." She leaned forward in the saddle. "That was the last of *my* gold, and it's coming out of *our* profits. And until *I* see those profits, *we're* partners."

Bertha sat back in her saddle and gently pulled on the reins to soothe the sidling gelding. Seemed he recognized her feelings and was a mite concerned. She'd had the cost of paying off her bills in Virginia City, setting up Mary and Betty for their journey to Arizona Territory, and getting supplies when she moved to the homestead. There was nothing left.

Henry, meanwhile, simply stared at her with narrowed eyes. The muscle in his cheek pulsed.

"Ma'am. The cattle need to be moved. You can't hold 'em in one place. They're grazing animals and need to keep moving and grazing. You and these fellows seem to think you can hold the herd here like it's a paddock."

Bertha felt her cheeks heat up. It wasn't often that a man could make her feel a fool, but Alsobrook had done it. It angered her, partly at herself because she didn't like to be in the wrong, and partly at him for pointing it out.

"Then it's a good thing you're done lazing in bed and available to work," she snapped.

She spun the horse around and put her fingers to her lips. She called out a piercing whistle. When Kit and Charlie both raised their heads, along with quite a few cows, she waved her arms to call them over.

"Who's tending down the hollow?" Henry asked.

Now it was Bertha's turn to grit her teeth. "No one."

There was no one else available, according to Kit. Bertha had left word with the hotel/barkeep, who turned out to be named "Rumor," to send anyone looking for work. But no one else had arrived yet. And no one even knew they'd have to wait for the cattle sale before getting paid.

Kit and Charlie rode up. Bertha introduced them to Henry. The man looked like death warmed over, but it was clear that wasn't going to slow him down. He had an aura of strong will that told you nothing was going to get in his way. Bertha suspected if they weren't at odds over the investment, they'd get along well.

"The reason the cattle are trying to scatter is they're looking for more to eat. There's a ridge just north of here, with a small creek at its base and a fine grazing pasture leading up to it. We'll move the herd there. That should keep them content for a couple of days."

Bertha, Kit, and Charlie nodded. It was hard for Bertha. She'd been in charge for years now and was used to it. It was hard to go back to doing as she was told. Even though she knew his directions were right, and his tone wasn't unreasonable, her hackles rose at bowing to the dictates of a man.

"Tomorrow, I'll start culling the herd for the ones I want to take to Virginia City."

Bertha wondered which ones he wanted to keep and how

that was going to affect their profits. What if they sold them all now? He might not like that, but it would take care of their partnership. But maybe she could be part of that deal. There'd be more risk, but it could mean the difference between enough money to survive the winter and enough to live on moving forward. Enough to achieve her dreams.

They started moving. Henry pulled alongside Bertha. "Tonight, we talk."

She nodded. Had he read her mind? She was usually adept at keeping her thoughts to herself, but Henry seemed to see right through her.

They had just gotten the herd to the pasture when a horseman was spotted in the distance. Perhaps it was someone come to work. Bertha sighed. She'd be glad if it was. Riding a herd was hard, dusty work. Her backside was getting sore, and she hadn't even been doing it for long.

She cut away from the herd and toward the rider. Henry came from the far side and trotted up beside her.

"I'll see about hiring him," he said.

"I'm the one who put out the call for hands," she said.

Henry glared at Bertha. "Ma'am. This is *my* spread."

They both continued toward the new rider.

It was Joshua Reynolds. He pulled up his horse and surveyed the cattle, Henry, and the dust covering Bertha. His nose twitched.

"Hello, Joshua," Bertha said. "What are you doing here?"

"I think the better question is 'What are *you* doing here?'" Reynolds glanced at Henry before returning his focus to Bertha. "Why are *you* out here riding the range?"

Bertha stared at him with her best you-are-misbehaving stare that usually caused a man to shut his trap and look abashed.

At the same time, Henry narrowed his eyes. "On my property, we treat a woman with more respect than that."

Joshua reddened. He tipped his hat and spoke again. "My pardon. I came out to check on Bertha. I just didn't expect her—you—to be out riding the range."

Bertha was mortified to be spoken to in such a way. She gripped the reins as her gelding danced under her. "I'm protecting my investment, Joshua. The cattle are my business until they're not anymore." She glared at Henry too. Let them both remember it.

Joshua gave her his winning smile that usually won her over, but today it made her grit her teeth. "Of course, but you've got to think of your reputation. You're turning over a new leaf. Living with men and riding the range…" He finished with a scrunch of his nose like he smelled something bad.

Years of practice kept Bertha from standing up in her stirrups and laying into Joshua with her tongue. She was about as angry as she could be. Angry that Joshua would try to tell her what to do. Angry because there was a modicum of truth in his words. Angry because Henry was witness to it all, and she didn't like looking bad in front of him, and she wasn't even sure why she cared.

Henry watched her, the corner of his mouth turned up, waiting to see if she would explode.

Joshua didn't see it at all. He turned to Henry. "Alsobrook, I'm Joshua Reynolds."

Henry nodded, his eyes surveying the new arrival from the tips of his fancy boots to the top of his crisp hat.

Bertha didn't think either man looked pleased to meet the other.

"Where exactly are you sleeping?" Joshua glanced between Henry and Bertha.

Henry's eyes narrowed. "You realize this is my land, right? It's no business of yours." His horse was as still as the man.

"Of course," said Joshua, his voice hard and intense. "I'm just thinking about Bertha's reputation."

Henry looked around in all directions. Except for Kit and the new hand, Charlie, there was no one but the three of them in sight.

Bertha stifled a smile.

Henry glanced at Bertha and returned his attention to Joshua. But before Henry could speak, Joshua addressed Bertha. "You are living on another man's spread. You're a new woman, now, or aren't you?"

Bertha inhaled a breath so deep she thought she might bust the buttons on her dress. Then she spoke in a voice so calm and quiet that both men had to lean in to hear her. "Why, yes. I am a new woman. But I'm not your woman. Yet." She was gratified by how both men's eyes widened in surprise. "I'm not much used to worrying about my reputation. Nor am I used to being told what to do." She let out her breath. "But I can see I need to start being more careful."

"Better start now," said Joshua. "Good practice for—uh, the future." He cut himself off.

Bertha turned her horse to look out over the cattle, though she didn't pay them any mind. This conversation left her feeling boxed in. She wanted a life in which she was not a tainted woman, but somehow, talking about circumscribing her behavior simply for the opinion of others—especially when there weren't any "others" around—felt wrong.

She looked back at the two men. Joshua was brushing dust off his coat sleeves. Then he looked up. "Come live in my hotel. That's for the best, I think. And we'll be nearer to each other." He smiled. He meant well, but her every instinct protested. She wasn't ready to give up her independence. She wasn't ready to trust in that future.

Henry didn't help. "If Bertha and the girls go with you, then Kit and Charlie can stay here." He tipped his head toward the two hands in the distance.

"Oh, no. I—" Bertha said, but then stopped. What could

she say? She couldn't leave Kit here alone. And she couldn't bring Kit into town, at least not as long as Kit was needed to help with the herd.

Well, there was nothing to it. She was staying.

"I'm staying here to keep track of my investment, and that's that."

Joshua sputtered. "You can't all sleep together like a litter of puppies."

Henry sighed. "I'll make a lean-to off the back of the cabin for Charlie, Kit, and me."

Bertha glanced across the herd at Kit, framed by high mountains and blue sky. She wished they could talk, but it was too late. She knew she had to tell the two men about Kit. Joshua, because if she had a future with him, there couldn't be secrets. And Henry, because it was his home, and he had a right to know.

"You need a spot for you and Charlie, Henry. Kit will sleep with the rest of us."

The two men were still for a moment. Then Joshua began to sputter again, and Henry raised his eyebrows so high they disappeared under his hat.

Bertha couldn't help but laugh. "I haven't been able to shock anyone since I moved out here. I guess I missed it." She turned her horse west. "Come along, and I'll explain."

The three walked their horses along the edge of the pasture. Bertha rode in the middle with the two men on either side of her.

"Kit is short for Catherine. Kit is a young woman, not the boy we've been pretending she is."

"Ah," said Henry as he gave one decisive nod, as though something had been answered for him.

"What?" yelped Joshua, his jaw hanging open.

"Is she yours?" asked Henry.

Joshua looked startled, glancing between Henry and Bertha. "Is she?" he demanded.

Bertha was taken aback by his vehemence. "I can't—I never—" She took a calming breath. "She is not mine by birth, but she's been with me for nigh on ten years, and I'm as much a mama as she's ever had in that time."

"Why is she acting a gal-boy?" Joshua was red in the face. "That isn't right."

Henry leveled a look at him. "Surely you can guess?"

Bertha pursed her lips. It seemed pretty obvious to her, too, but Joshua was perhaps too upset to think clearly.

"Kit came to me when she was twelve. Her parents died of typhoid in the California gold fields. There was no other family to speak of. Since I was the only woman around, the girl was brought to me. Despite her young age, and looking even younger, there was a bit too much interest in her, so I asked her to dress as a boy. We moved to different camps where no one knew us, or that she was a girl.

"It's one of the reasons I moved to Montana Territory. It allowed us to go where no one knew her and to change her age back a few more years too."

Joshua was turning purple. "And in the brothel? Was he a —? Was she a—? How many men did you fool?" He choked.

Henry leaned forward in the saddle, just to look at Joshua with disgust. "You damn fool. Bertha didn't let Kit get involved in that part of the business. Bertha protected the girl so she wouldn't have to. I don't know Bertha so well as you claim to, but you've got a bee in your bonnet for a damn fool reason."

Bertha felt gratefulness surge through her. She couldn't remember the last time a man spoke up in her defense. The closest was when men defended the brothel from Bible-thumpers as a necessary part of life.

But this was about her as a person. She smiled at Henry.

He looked startled. She tried to tone it down, but it was too late.

She glanced at Joshua and saw anger flash across his face. Joshua reached out and grabbed Bertha's reins, halting her horse. "We're talking about a future together, and you're holding secrets."

"Now, Joshua," Bertha said, but he held his hand up to stop her.

"We'll talk about this another time," he said in a low voice, releasing her reins, "in private. Here, take this letter I brought out." He reached into his pocket and pulled out a letter that he shoved at her.

Joshua spurred his horse and galloped away.

Bertha watched his direction long after he was out of sight. She was, once again, confused by a mix of emotions. Anger that these men wanted to make her do as they thought best, not letting her make her own decisions. Relief that she had revealed Kit's secret. It was time for the young woman hidden under a boy's clothes to come forth. Fear for that young woman too. Fear that Bertha's own future as a respectable wife could be in jeopardy. And bitterness that after all she had overcome, she could be ruined by the fate of these skinny cows and whatever gossip someone cared to spread.

But perhaps Joshua was right. It was time to start behaving like the woman she proposed to be. Even out on a nearly empty ranch.

Bertha suppressed her thoughts when she saw Alsobrook watching her, his mouth set in a hard line. That set her off. What right did he have to be annoyed? He might not like having a former madam and ladies of the night at his home, but that was just too bad. She knew she was riding roughshod over his life, but she didn't have a choice, and that was that. At least she was helping him on the ranch for their investment. She'd had men take over her life before, and what she was doing was a lot less terrible and permanent than what they'd done to her.

She opened her mouth to give him a what-for, but before she could speak, Henry said, "Let's go," and began trotting toward Kit.

Bertha took a deep breath. She spurred her horse past Henry's. She wanted to be the one to tell Kit that the cat was out of the bag. She was still in charge of her own life, and she wasn't giving that up. Yet.

CHAPTER 8

Henry was annoyed. And angry. And frustrated.

He used his shovel to pry the stone out of the ground and then lifted it onto the low sledge. His muscles burned with the exertion. The horses might not be too keen on dragging a sledge full of rocks back to the cabin, but it sure beat breaking an axle in the wagon under the weight.

First, there was the situation with Bertha. He was annoyed as all hell, but not at her. Or at least, not entirely at her. He wasn't too keen on the way she had moved onto his homestead and into his cabin without his agreement. Of course, he wouldn't have agreed. But he understood she'd had little choice.

On the other hand, there was something to be said about a partner helping out too. Cooking breakfast. Riding the range. Tending the gardens. Or, since it was late fall, at least digging up the last of the root vegetables.

And she was mighty beautiful, to boot.

After being on his own for so long, to have people around him, though not all as pretty as Bertha, to work with and even just to talk to, was a pleasure. It could be mighty lonely on a homestead all by himself. He'd been imagining a family on his ranch, and this ragbag of people was nothing like he had imagined, but it caused that empty space in him to feel a bit less empty.

But these weren't the right folk—the family of his choosing—and that was annoying too. He had all the burden of a family, but it wasn't his.

When he'd left this morning, Eugenie was still abed, moaning something fierce. She'd been sickly all week, casting up most of what she ate and complaining about headaches and pain. Bertha had sent Kit to town for the doctor. There was nothing Henry could do, but he wished he could, seeing how the worry etched Bertha's face when she thought no one was looking.

But most annoying of all was the way Joshua Reynolds kept showing up. Henry slammed the shovel so forcefully into the ground that the wooden shaft bowed and flexed. The man was coming by for chitchat and courting. He ought to be a politician with that flannelmouth. But Bertha liked all the sweet talk and the promises of the easy life waiting for her in St. Louis.

Henry grunted as he struggled to roll the heavy stone over to the sled. It wasn't an easy life here. And Henry might not like having Bertha as a partner, but damn it, he needed every hand he could get right now. She might not have cattle experience, but she was a hardworking woman who did what she had to do. He admired her a bit, even if she was a pain in his side. Perhaps what he admired the most was that she kept so positive and cheerful despite all the setbacks in her life. And Joshua's visits were pure interruption as far as Henry was concerned.

Equally annoying, Henry had to admit to himself, was that this man seemed to have lots of money but didn't seem to work very hard. Joshua bought a young steer yesterday, and when Henry asked when he wanted it butchered, Joshua said, "I'll use the fellow in town." Henry knew the butcher in town was half as good as Henry and charged twice as much, but it didn't seem to matter to Joshua. He was more concerned with the pomade in his hair.

Henry looked at the pile of stones on the sledge. The horses shifted in their traces. They could pull a deal more weight, but Henry was beat. He had blisters on his hands and a sore back. His muscles jittered with fatigue. Already today, he'd run the cattle to the upper pasture, hauled wash water for the womenfolk, and quarried this collection of stone. He didn't get half done what he'd normally have accomplished, but his body wasn't fully recovered from the scarlet fever and the ride up from Texas.

Henry walked up to the heads of the horses and began leading them down the trail. The horses heaved against their heavy load, slowly dragging the sledge along.

He ran the calculations in his head once again. He knew he could sell the cattle at a decent price, once they were fattened up a bit more, and pay back Bertha; it was getting through until then. He'd thought about sticking to the original plan and running the cows out to the Virginia City area. They needed fattening, but he could do it and pay off Bertha in full. She'd take her crazy brood and leave.

But the cost... he wouldn't have enough cattle left to develop a decent herd of his own.

If he waited till spring, he'd have calves, both to sell and to keep. He might have to give a bit more of the profit to Bertha, to incent her to wait, but then he'd be set for the following year with a decent-sized herd.

And beautiful Big Bertha would be living in his cabin all winter.

And Henry would be stuck sleeping in the lean-to.

And Joshua would be coming round all winter to court her and irritate Henry.

That settled it in Henry's mind. He'd take the cattle to

Virginia City in a few weeks, pay off his debt and send Bertha and her flock packing.

Henry nodded to himself. It was the right decision. He looked ahead to the cabin. Bertha was tending an open fire in the yard, stirring a pot of something that would be tonight's supper. The smoke drifted up into the air, caught by a light breeze that drew it east. Bertha hung the long-handled spoon from the end of the spit. She stretched her back and tucked a loose lock of hair behind her ear.

She hadn't complained about cooking in the yard. Only once, the other day, she'd said to him while they'd all sat outside on a cool evening after supper, "I wonder when you're planning to finish that fireplace. It's going to get a mite cold soon." She'd raised that eyebrow of hers, and Kit had smothered a laugh.

Well, here he was with another load of stone for the fireplace. That oughta please her.

Henry led the horses round to the side of the cabin. He halted them and walked back to unload the stones as close to where he'd need them as he could manage.

Bertha approached, looking Henry up and down. "Perhaps this should wait till Charlie gets back. You look winded."

Henry grunted as he hauled a rock up. "No point in waiting. It's got to get done." He didn't look up to see her expression, but her silence spoke of her disapproval.

He paused to lean against the horse's flank and catch his breath. He hated having to rest, especially in front of Bertha.

She stood on the far side of the horses, gently petting the bay's shoulder and brushing away dust. She'd taken to simple hairstyles, but the kitchen work and laundry caused her hair to steam and curl around her face in a way no curling iron could replicate. It made her look sweet and soft like she deserved to feel. She continued to stroke the horse's shoulder, glancing occasionally at Henry.

He began to wish he was the horse.

"I can take the cattle to town in a few weeks and have your money for you. You'll be free to live in town again," he bit out.

Henry expected to see Bertha flash that brilliant smile. Instead, she stilled, staring at her hand on the horse's side. Her lips moved slightly, as though she were about to speak, but no sound emerged.

Before he knew what he was doing, Henry filled up the silence. "If you're willing to wait until spring, I can pay you a bit more of the profit."

Bertha's head shot up, a look of surprise on her face. Probably no more surprised than he was, thought Henry. What was he doing?

"But if you're going to stay all winter, I'll be charging room and board. Twenty dollars per month. Each." He spoke gruffly. No need for her to expect a holiday.

The corner of Bertha's mouth tipped up, just the slightest smile. "Of course, we can't pay you until you pay me in the spring."

Henry nodded. "I know it."

Bertha stepped away from the horse after one last pet and headed back around the cabin.

Henry watched her skirts sway and almost didn't realize she was looking over her shoulder at him. When their eyes caught, her smile grew.

"Come warm up by the fire when you're done here."

He nodded, and she disappeared around the corner. If he'd had the energy, he would have kicked himself. As it was, all he could do was keep hauling rocks off the skid and onto the pile he was growing. He should have finished their deal as planned. Sent her and her girls on their way. That poor girl, Eugenie, she wasn't going to be a help on the ranch anyway.

He was not going to admit to himself that he liked having Bertha around. How was he supposed to live with someone so desirable and not touch her, anyway? He stuffed that thought down deep. After the last rock was unloaded, he led the horses and the sledge away. He unhooked the sledge and removed the harnesses from the horses. He gave them each a pet on the nose and then a swat on the flank.

"Go get some grass, boys. Good work today."

He watched them trot off before heading back to the fire and Bertha. He was hot and sweaty, but the cool evening air sent a chill down his back. Bertha was right that they'd be needing the fireplace sooner rather than later.

Originally, he'd planned to have a fire ring in the dirt floor and a hole in the ceiling for the smoke to escape. That would have worked for the first winter with just him and maybe a hand or two to share the cabin. But there were too many skirts floating around to have a fire in the middle of the floor. And he and Charlie would freeze to death in the lean-to unless he could warm it up. Putting in the fireplace and then moving the lean-to to the back of the chimney would let the warm stones take the edge off the cold Montana winter. For now though, Henry would stand by the warm fire outside in the yard.

Bertha was scooping stew into a bowl. She slid a spoon into it and handed it to Henry as he walked up.

"I hope you don't mind eating out here."

"Think your boyfriend will be upset if we eat inside?" The words popped out of his mouth before he knew it. He shoved a spoonful of stew in his mouth before he could say anything else without using his brainpan first and nearly scalded his tongue.

Bertha's eyes were scalding too. "Eugenie is resting inside. Mary and Kit are taking turns reading to her."

Henry nodded and tried to pretend his eyes weren't watering from the pain in his mouth. When he finally swallowed, he asked, "Did Kit find the doc in town?"

Bertha looked at the cabin, as though she could see through the walls to the young women inside.

"She did. Eugenie… she's not well. The doctor thinks she has something called toxemia. He's only ever read about it. But she—" Bertha's voice caught. "She's even having trouble with her seeing. Things are turning blurry."

Henry stopped with his spoon halfway to his mouth. "Blurry? Because of the baby?"

Bertha nodded. "Some kind of blood poisoning that a woman carrying can get."

"Is she going to lose the baby?" he asked.

"Likely. Or worse." Bertha bent down to poke at the fire, hiding her face.

Henry felt like he ought to do something, but there wasn't much he could do. He felt foolish standing there with a spoon hanging in front of his face, so he stuck it in his mouth and kept eating. After a few moments, Bertha stood up.

"There is a bit of good news."

"Let's hear it."

"That letter Joshua brought. It was a letter for Lily from her young Swede. Harald proposed marriage." The pride on Bertha's face was evident. Her caring for the girls, the fear and the pride, it couldn't be stronger if she was their true mother.

He looked at Bertha in the fading light, the glow of the fire flashing in her blond hair. She didn't need fancy doodad dresses and hats to look beautiful. It shone from inside her.

She was a truly kind woman. Bertha would make any man a good partner. Some men wouldn't look past her past, but Henry knew she'd had to overcome some tough stuff to get where she was.

And that was why she deserved to go back East with Joshua, to a life of leisure where no one looked down on her. Not a ranch life where her back would ache and her hands would be red and cracked.

Bertha would leave in the spring. But how, Henry

wondered, could he ask any woman to live this difficult life on the frontier?

He turned away, looking up at the mountains. Though the valley and foothills were still gold and brown, the mountaintops had snow already settled in between the evergreen trees. There was a long winter ahead.

"I guess we ought to take Lily to her man before snow makes the journey too difficult. We'll take a few steers with us and get the winter supplies."

He wondered if, once back in Virginia City, Bertha would want to stay.

Bertha placed a small gray stone, the last one, into place. Henry and Charlie had already spent hours digging in the half-frozen earth. They'd lowered Eugenie's body, wrapped in a sheet, into the hole. They'd shoveled the dirt back in and placed the larger stones over the grave.

Henry had offered to stay and help her, but Bertha had asked to be alone. He left to go make a wooden cross with Eugenie's name carved into it.

For Bertha, arranging the stones on top of the grave was her final job for Eugenie. Eugenie had always been so neat and tidy with her own self-grooming and the room she slept and worked in. She would appreciate having a neat grave, if a person could ever appreciate such a thing.

Bertha stood back and surveyed the gravesite. She picked up a stick and stuck it in the ground, right where she wanted Henry to place the marker. Tears filled her eyes.

A week after the doctor had visited, seven days of pain and fear for Eugenie, she and the baby inside her had passed. Such a hard life cut off so early. Bertha wiped at the tears on her cheeks.

How easily this could have been her! Since those many years ago when Bertha's life had taken a terrible turn, so many things could have killed her. That none of them had was shocking. What made her so sad though was not that she herself could have died, but how many other girls and women had: from the trauma of losing a baby early, to death in child-birth, to disease and violence. If Bertha was the exception, Eugenie was the rule in the wild frontier.

Bertha's hands balled into fists. She wanted so terribly to forget how hard life was, to go back to that time before she was sixteen, when she was young and innocent. She thought back to the small farm she'd been raised on, to the family who had sheltered her from all the terrible things life could offer. Perhaps that had been wrong. Perhaps if she'd better under-stood the dangers of the world, she would have been better adept at dealing with them.

But Lily—she hadn't been sheltered, and she still ended up on the same road as Bertha. That said, Lily knew what an opportunity she had with young Harald. True love and a rare chance to get out of the life working in the night. Lily, thought Bertha, would know to her dying day how to appreciate what she had gained. She and Harald were going to continue on to Oregon and homestead there. Lily had said, "I'm sorry, Bertha, for I appreciate all you've done for me, but when I leave, I'll be cutting all ties. I'm going to start a new life, and no one there, 'cepting my Harald, will ever know what I been through and what I done."

Even though that was what Bertha planned to do with Joshua, it hurt something fierce to hear it from Lily.

But Eugenie, she wouldn't get the opportunity to redeem herself. There was no one to mourn her here but Bertha, Kit, and Lily. Bertha couldn't even send word to Mary and Betty in Arizona, for she didn't yet know where in the territory they were.

Eugenie had finally, near the end, told Bertha where to write to her family.

Bertha had been leaning over the young woman, tucking in the blankets. A path of dried tears streaked across Eugenie's hollow cheeks into her brown hair.

"My folks weren't too good with the mistakes of the living, but they were pretty good at praying for lost souls. Maybe they'll pray for me, finally," Eugenie had whispered.

Bertha sank to her knees onto the cold, hard ground. She squeezed her hands together, and then her eyes. More tears leaked out, turning cold in the crisp air.

She had two choices, it seemed, because she couldn't hide out on Henry's ranch forever. She could keep going like Mary and Betty, and like Eugenie, end up dead, one way or another. Or she could be like Lily and start over in a new town, pretending her past didn't exist. That was what she was planning with Joshua. She'd have to leave Montana Territory and the friends she'd made. But what about Kit? She could never—would never—banish Kit from her life. Joshua would have to understand that.

Bertha wished she could find a way to get Kit happily settled before she headed east in the spring. Kit's upbringing had been unconventional, but surely there was a place for the young woman in this territory.

Bertha placed her hands over her face, feeling the damp of her cheeks. *If only there was a place for Bertha.*

VIRGINIA CITY

Bertha stood on the boardwalk, looking at the place where her home and business had been. The burnt shell she had last seen was gone. Already a new building was in place. It was a mix of stacked logs and cut wood not yet weathered to gray. It was a saloon, and from the sounds coming from inside, a rather rowdy one. She wondered if the lawyer next door thought this was an improvement over the brothel.

She was to meet Henry soon. They were going to have a celebratory supper at a restaurant down the street. She'd stood at Lily's side this morning when the young woman had married Harald, both smiling from ear to ear. Henry had been off arranging the sale of the steers they'd brought to town with them. Then she'd gone to the mercantile to sell some potatoes and purchase supplies for winter. She'd so enjoyed catching up with Reg and Josie there.

But here and now, she was surprised at the loss she felt. The loss of Lily, of the friends she missed here in Virginia City, even of the loss of her old home.

She'd always planned to sell the building, but somehow a part of her was gone with it. There was plenty in her history that she'd like to forget, but of this she'd been proud. Proud of her independence. Proud of the fact that she more than survived, she thrived. And she helped others along the way.

She suspected Joshua wouldn't like her visiting this old place.

"Is that you, Big Bertha?"

Bertha turned to see a grizzled old miner with one black eye and the other patched, leaning on a crutch, holding a shaking hand out.

"Cadoc!" Bertha stepped up to him and took his hand in hers and gently squeezed. "What happened to you? You look like you've been run through a rocker!"

"Never mind about that, Bertha. A claim jumper tried to end my career." He drew his shoulders back in pride. "But you oughta see *him*! Ha!" He gripped her fingers tighter. "You're a sight for sore eyes. We miss you and your girls."

Bertha's heart swelled and cracked at the same time. Here was a sweet old man, hair more salt than pepper, who had visited her girls to play cards in secret and tell stories of his upbringing in a coal-mining town in Wales. "I'd rather look across the table at a pretty girl than at the old dogs found round here," he'd said.

It was silly, but she was extra glad she'd dressed up for Lily's wedding. It felt good to be back in her element.

"I miss you, too, Cadoc." Bertha leaned in and whispered, "You were my best bridge partner."

He cackled. "Don't I know it!"

"You look the worse for wear, hon," she said gently. "You can't be working your claim right now."

He shook his head. "I'm guarding it, but I-I…can't do much right now. I'm sorry, Bertha. It'll be a bit before I can pay you back."

Bertha looked around, as though a solution to both their problems might appear. She saw Henry watching her from a distance. She must be overdue at the restaurant. His serious expression didn't tell her what he thought of her encounter with Cadoc. She looked up at the saloon's porch roof and suddenly remembered J.B. helping her down the night of the fire.

"Don't you worry about that. You ought to go speak with J.B. Wood. He knows mines, and he's honest as the winter is cold. He'll have an idea to help you out…until you're back in the saddle, of course."

There was a long pause, and Bertha caught sight of a sheen of tears cross the Welshman's eye. He squeezed her hand tight.

"Thank you, Big Bertha. You're a damn fine woman."

"Go on now, Cadoc. You're making me blush." She leaned over to kiss his cheek. "You take care of yourself, you hear?"

She watched him limp away in the direction of J.B.'s cabin. She wondered if Vanderbilt had such trouble getting his investments to pay out. After a moment, she realized Henry had arrived to stand beside her, still and watchful.

"He doesn't look too good."

"No," she said, "just a tad better than you looked when you arrived back home from the cattle drive."

Henry smiled. "That so?"

Bertha smiled back.

"Are you ready to eat, ma'am?"

"I'm ready to celebrate," she said, flashing a smile, determined to put her losses behind her. She put her arm through Henry's, and they walked to the restaurant. Along the way they saw three carved squash and two men wearing masks, reminding them it was All Hallows' Eve. It was easy to lose track of dates when living out on the ranch.

Twice they were stopped by locals who knew Bertha and asked where she had been.

After they were seated and had ordered, they began to discuss what urgent chores were left on the ranch to do before winter moved in. While they waited for food, the bartender brought them their celebratory whiskeys.

"I'll be glad when you've finished the fireplace, Henry. It's getting a mite cold at night."

Henry opened his mouth to reply when they were interrupted by a small gold nugget that was tossed onto the table.

Bertha and Henry looked up to see a man approaching them. He had a greasy beard and an ill-fitting suit that made him look like a failed bank clerk. "When you're done with that one, I want you in the back room."

Bertha stilled, and the noise around them quieted. She couldn't tell if her skin had paled from shock or reddened from embarrassment. Her time spent in the Gallatin Valley at Henry's ranch...well, her guard had fallen. She glanced at Henry and saw a muscle tick in his jaw. He looked at her, assessing, and then back at the stranger who swayed with drink.

Henry shot up to standing, his chair screeching. In two

steps, he was in front of the man, his hand wrapped around the man's collar and lifting him to his toes.

"You will apologize to the lady for your disrespect."

"I will not—"

Henry shook the man hard. He stared hard into the man's eyes. "Shut your big bazoo and listen. You will apologize to the lady, or I will beat the tar out of you. And then you will apologize."

The man's eyes flared open. He gawked around and saw that none of his friends were stepping forward to help him. In fact, some of the other patrons appeared to be lining up to add to his beating and were ready to stop his friends from aiding him, if they were even so inclined. The man looked at Bertha, but she said nothing. She wasn't going to make it easier on him.

She'd had men fight over her in the past. She'd had some men disrespect her, too, and she'd defended herself as best she could. It was one of the reasons she'd opened her own brothel, so that she and her girls could kick out any man who disrespected them.

But it had been a long time…a very long time…since a man had stood up and defended her loud and clear. And that several men stood ready to back Henry up… she didn't know which emotion swirling inside of her to focus on.

The man nodded as best he could, considering Henry's fist was balled up under his chin. Henry let go, and the man dropped three inches. He rubbed his throat for a moment and then, when Henry made a low noise—a growl, really—the man looked at Bertha. He tipped his hat.

"Sorry, ma'am. I mistook you for"—another growl from Henry had the man taking a step back—"for someone else, ma'am. Uh, I'll be going." He glanced at the gold nugget at the table. Henry reached over, scooped it up and tossed it to the bartender.

"There's a couple of newlyweds at the hotel," Henry said. "Will you see that Harald and Lily get this wedding present?"

The bartender nodded and tipped an imaginary hat.

"Right," the man mumbled. He grabbed his coat off a hook on the wall and ran out the front door.

The silence continued for the merest bit more, and then conversations resumed.

Henry looked around, meeting and holding several sets of eyes before he was satisfied there would be no more trouble. He took his seat again.

What struck Bertha at that moment was the way Henry looked at her. He was concerned for how she felt. Was she hurt or embarrassed or scared? There wasn't a bit in the look that said she deserved such attention or that it was her fault or even to be expected. Whatever her past sins, he was worried about her here and now.

Maybe it was because they were business partners.

Maybe they were becoming friends.

"Thank you," she said. She lifted up her whiskey to toast him.

Henry nodded and clinked his glass to hers. He finished off his whiskey and looked around the room again. He was, Bertha realized, protecting her.

CHAPTER 10

NOVEMBER, MADISON VALLEY

"I'm thinking we'd best stop off at the Hisers' ranch," said Henry. The wagon lurched in a dip, and Bertha, seated on the bench beside him, tipped into his shoulder. "We've got a ways to go still, but with the wind whipping up and the lateness of the afternoon, I don't think we'll make it far before dark."

They'd camped on the way out with Lily and the steers. They'd spent the night before Lily's wedding in a Virginia City hotel and again last night, but no one had been impressed with the cleanliness of the rooms. They'd planned to leave early this morning, but only one mile out of town, one of the horses had thrown a shoe. They'd returned to Virginia City to visit the blacksmith before turning around and heading back out again.

The road north over the Madison Mountains had been steep and slow going. They'd gone about twenty miles, and it was already 2 p.m. The sun was heading toward the tops of the Madisons in the west, while the Gallatin Mountains to the east were looming large. The wind coming through the valley blew cold.

Bertha straightened and pulled the blanket tighter around her legs. "If the choice is a ranch house or camping in those mountains over there, I'll take the house."

That was the only thing Bertha had said to indicate she noticed the cold or was uncomfortable traveling in the wagon. They were able to travel more quickly going home because they weren't herding cattle anymore. The wagon was empty of potatoes and Lily, but it was still heavy since they'd loaded it with supplies. Without Eugenie and Lily, there was still Henry, Bertha, Kit, and Charlie to get through the winter.

Bertha had been quiet since they left Virginia City. She seemed to be enjoying the scenery, speaking occasionally about it but mostly lost in her own thoughts.

She probably had a lot to think about. That man at the saloon—Henry had wanted to grind him to a pulp. It was only because his mama had taught him to never fight in front of a lady that he hadn't. And Bertha was a lady. A lady who had fallen on hard times, obviously, but not one to give up. She was a strong woman.

He remembered how her hand had shook, ever so slightly, when she lifted up her glass for their toast yesterday. She acted so tough, but she was vulnerable underneath that brassy exterior.

"I'm sorry you had to go through that yesterday." The words popped out of his mouth before he'd thought about it. He hoped she wouldn't be offended by him bringing it up.

Bertha gave him a wry smile. "It's not the first time and won't be the last, I suspect." She studied his face for a moment, and Henry felt his cheeks redden. "Thank you for defending me." She looked like she wanted to say more, but after a moment he realized she wasn't going to.

"I came out here to make my fortune, but that doesn't mean I left all decencies back in the States. Too many men, without their womenfolk to keep an eye on them, act like animals."

Bertha nodded, her eyes fixed on the distant mountains. "Even the womenfolk sometimes forget their decencies out here."

Henry watched Bertha out of the corner of his eye. She continued to stare into the distance, her hands playing with the folds of the blanket.

"I came West when I was sixteen." She glanced at Henry and then looked away, talking to the empty land around her. "Typhoid ran through our town, killing lots of folks, including my mother and father."

"I'm sorry," said Henry.

"I had a beau. We wanted to marry, but both our parents had wanted us to wait until we turned eighteen. His family decided to head to California, to the gold fields. My aunt and uncle let me travel with his family, as we begged them to let me do, with the promise from his parents that we'd marry as soon as I turned eighteen."

Henry pictured a young Bertha walking alongside a Conestoga wagon, perhaps holding hands with her young man.

"One evening, not long after they staked a claim, I was out gathering kindling."

Henry's gut clenched. He was afraid he knew what Bertha was going to say.

"There were five men. Men who found it was easier to rob miners than to be miners. I screamed, but no one came."

A sheen of tears glistened in Bertha's eyes, but not one fell. The horses danced in their traces, feeling the clenching of Henry's hands through the reins.

"My beau wanted nothing to do with me anymore, and his parents…well, their decencies involved separating the indecent me from their decent son."

"I want to punch someone right now," Henry said with a growl.

Bertha choked with a laugh, and the tears disappeared from her eyes.

"It's long done, Henry," she said. Henry couldn't believe this beautiful woman was trying to comfort him.

"They ran me off with nothing but one dress and two biscuits to eat. I…" She hesitated, glancing at Henry.

Henry imagined a young girl in California Territory, already suffering from an attack and then being abandoned because of it. Grown men often didn't survive in the wilds with supplies, never mind without them. He felt a conflict of emotions inside him. Anger at that family. Burning hot anger. Sadness for the mortification of a young Bertha. And, strangely, pride that she'd come so far.

"I eventually made it to a mining camp. There wasn't but one way for a girl to make money so she could eat."

He gathered the reins in one hand and placed the other over Bertha's hand resting on her lap. He squeezed gently. "I'm glad you survived."

There was a world of words more he wanted to say, but he didn't know how to say them, or if he even had the right to do so.

Bertha turned her hand over. He threaded his fingers through hers. She leaned toward him and rested her head on his shoulder.

When they crossed the creek, they had to separate hands. Henry braced his boots on the footboard and used both hands on the reins. Bertha clasped the buckboard seat so she didn't roll off when the wagon lurched over the rocks or slid sideways in a sandy spot. When they were across, they didn't bring their hands back together.

. . .

THEY APPROACHED THE RANCH HOUSE. IT WAS A RAMBLING building, already built onto twice.

"They have so many folks stopping over between Bozeman and Virginia City that they've started charging as a hotel," Henry said. "I met Milo and Dorothea when they were living in Virginia City. Milo had a small mine—it never paid out— and we used to commiserate about that backbreaking work. When they moved out here, I only got to see them when they came to town for supplies." He pointed to a woman stepping out of the house, wiping her hands on her apron. "There's Dorothea."

The short, round woman with a braid crisscrossing her head waved as they approached.

"Halloo, Henrik. Eet ees gut to see you. Gut you bring your friend." She pointed to the sky. "Night coming. Welcome. Welcome."

Bertha smiled and swung herself off the wagon.

"I'll put up the horses and be along." He flicked the reins but traveled only a few steps before Dorothea stopped him.

"No, no, Henrik. The boys will get it." She reached up and swung the clacker of a bell hanging off the porch roof. She turned to Bertha and said proudly, "I haf two boys."

Moments later two boys came running around the corner of the house. They ran straight to their mother. "Ja, Mama?" the elder, who looked about fourteen, said.

"Bring die Pferde in die Scheune," Helga said.

"Ja," the boys said. They trotted over to the wagon. Henry hopped down as the boys scrambled up.

"Hello, Friedrich and Rolf," said Henry.

"No, sir! Call us Freddy and Ralph. We're going to be Americans someday."

Henry laughed. Bertha stood on the porch, a sweet smile

lighting up her face. Wearing her simple dress, without all the ornamentation she'd worn in town as Big Bertha, her hair still piled on her head—but without artificial curls—she looked like a beautiful, sexy ranch wife. Imagine coming home to her each day. Henry thought of Joshua and struggled to keep a scowl off his face. Joshua would give her a fancy house in a big town where Bertha wouldn't struggle to survive like the folks here in Montana Territory. She could get whatever she wanted from the market without a month's wait. She didn't have to worry about Indians or bands of rovers or whether there was a doctor or a preacher within fifty miles.

Or being disrespected for her past.

The boys drove the wagon across the yard to the barn. Henry walked up on the porch. He leaned down to give the little woman a kiss on the cheek.

"Hello, Dorothea. It's good to see you."

"You are too skinny, Henrik!" She hugged him and then looked at him archly. "Introduce me to your lady."

"Dorothea, this is my friend Mrs. Bertha Banks. Bertha, this is Mrs. Dorothea Hiser."

The two women smiled at each other. Bertha's expression turned to surprise when her hand was grabbed.

"Mrs. Banks, you come wit me. I haf a fire inside to warm you." Dorothea dragged Bertha inside.

Henry couldn't stop smiling. It wasn't often that Bertha didn't have control of any situation. He followed them in.

Dorothea set about making a pot of coffee. Bertha settled into the chair by the fire as directed.

"Henrik, you tell me. I haf been learning to read English." Dorothea pointed to the newspaper resting on the table. "Wat is this Tanksgiving that is coming this month?"

"A national day of giving thanks."

"That is gut, but why?"

"The first Thanksgiving was to celebrate the survival of the Pilgrims—those were early settlers—back in 1621."

"So you Americans haf celebrated every year since then?"

"No, ma'am. Some folks didn't think a country that separated Church and State should have a national holiday thanking God. But three years ago, President Lincoln wanted to give thanks because the Union victory at Gettysburg turned the tide of the War Between the States. Folks weren't so concerned about the separation then, I guess."

Dorothea nodded. "Ja, it ees hard to not tink about God when you are at war. When we left Prussia I pray all time we escape the soldiers."

Bertha sat quietly in the chair next to the fire. Henry was used to Bertha dominating a room, and while his eyes were still drawn to her constantly, it was not her big personality that did it. Her eyes followed Dorothea around, a yearning look that made Henry feel pity. He realized Bertha had lost her own loving mother and the woman she had thought would be her mother-in-law when she was only a few years older than Dorothea's boys.

Dorothea poured a cup of coffee and brought it to Bertha. "I tink it is a good holiday. Life ees hard, but we haf much to be tankful for, ja?"

Bertha nodded mutely.

"Now, I get potatoes from the root cellar. You stay and be warm. You, also, Henrik."

Dorothea busied herself out of the cabin.

"You look bemused," said Henry.

Bertha gestured around the room and to the door that Dorothea had just exited.

"It's been a long time since a woman invited me into her home and treated me so kindly."

Henry paused as he reached for a log for the fire. It made sense, but it wasn't something he'd thought of. Despite the trouble in the bar, he had known Dorothea would welcome Bertha. But what if he'd brought Big Bertha, brothel owner, to Dorothea's door instead of Mrs. Banks, struggling pioneer?

"It's rather pleasant," said Bertha.

That, thought Henry, was an understatement if he ever heard one.

"Dorothea welcomes everyone."

"Perhaps," said Bertha as she stood up. "After sitting on that wagon bench all day, I don't want to sit anymore. I'm going to find Dorothea and see if I can help her prepare dinner."

Henry watched Bertha walk out. She didn't put the same swing in her skirt as she did back when he first met her in Virginia City, but she had a natural sway that he couldn't take his eyes off. That scene in Virginia City, it had raised feelings in him—feelings for Bertha—that he had no right to feel.

Henry fiddled with the fire, half banking it since no one else was there to enjoy it. Then he stepped out to see if the boys needed his help putting up the horses. He'd see if he could find Dorothea's husband, Milo, and help him. He ought to not stand around sniffing at Bertha's skirts.

Out in the barn, Freddy and Ralph had already unharnessed the horses under the supervision of their father. Henry took over brushing them while they ate their grain, sending the boys to finish their other chores. In the dim light, with the quiet lowing of cows and the sound of the horses munching, he found himself telling Milo about Bertha's situation. Not in detail, but about their business deal and how a fire drove her from Virginia City and how she would stay at his ranch for the winter.

Milo listened while he forked hay out of the loft for the cows. "She sounds like quite a woman. A gut ranch wife. You like her."

Henry did like Bertha, but she wasn't his to like. "She's heading back to the States in the spring. With her fiancé."

Milo hung the pitchfork between two nails on the wall. "But I tink she ees not married yet. Ja, Henry?"

Henry thought about beautiful Bertha. Sassy Bertha. Loving Bertha who collected strays wherever she went. He wondered how Joshua would deal with that back in St. Louis. Bertha wasn't going to stop helping people or protecting girls and old men.

"A gut woman at your side…tink about it."

Henry looked out the barn door toward the house. Bertha and Dorothea were emerging from a root cellar. Bertha held a basket, and Dorothea's apron was loaded with potatoes. They were grinning. Bertha's head tipped back in laughter at something Dorothea said, the fading afternoon light shining gold in her hair.

Think about it, indeed.

CHAPTER 11

GALLATIN VALLEY

Bertha strained to make out the cabin in the distance. As Henry drove the wagon over the last foothill leading to the ranch, Henry's land opened up in front of them. The cabin, situated near the creek, a kitchen garden, and the potato field surrounding it were nestled amongst the golden-brown fall grasses. The barn, half built into a hillock, was barely noticeable except as a squarish contour in the valley. The paddock was empty, and there was no sign of Kit or Charlie. It was all framed by the beautiful Bridger Mountains, already tipped with snow.

Home. Though she had lived there only a month, Bertha found the word sliding through her head with a gentle sigh. This was, she realized, what she had expected of her life all those years ago when she had first headed West. Visiting Dorothea and her family, staying at their hotel-home, seeing the love and companionship—the common struggle shared—it brought up thoughts she had buried long ago. Since they'd left the Hisers' ranch yesterday morning, she'd thought of little else.

Sure, she and her beau's family had gone to California first. But she and her intended had thought to head north to Oregon to farm after they struck it rich in the goldfields. Their hopeful naivete made Bertha wince. In any case, she had imagined a small house with a porch, a barn for the horses, a kitchen garden, and fields of whatever crop her husband had deemed appropriate for the landscape they settled in. They would have children.

Bertha felt a stab in her heart. She had never been with child. She suspected the injuries from the attack when she was sixteen had been the cause. She could have had children the age of Dorothea's if she'd married her beau all those years ago.

She wondered if Joshua wanted to have children. She would have to address this with him.

The wagon lurched in a rut, and she slid into Henry. He glanced at her, and the corners of his mouth curved in a hint of a smile. She'd told Henry her story, without premeditation, and his response had been…well, the best she could hope for. Would Joshua feel the same?

She straightened her shoulders. It didn't matter. The past was the past, and she couldn't change it. She had decided a long time ago that she would find a way to go back to living in a proper city and end the hardship that living on the frontier required.

The wagon came to a halt outside the cabin. It was very quiet after the hubbub of Virginia City. Henry put on the brake, jumped down to tie the horses to the hitching rail and then came around to assist Bertha down. He stretched his arms over his head, wincing slightly.

"Lordy, I'm stiff as a board," Henry said as he held out his hand to Bertha. She quirked an eyebrow at him, and they both laughed.

They began to unload the wagon of the supplies purchased in Virginia City.

Then a voice called, "Hello!"

Bertha and Henry looked around. There in the distance they saw Kit and Joshua riding toward them.

The two riders approached and dismounted. Kit stood, holding her horse, whose tired head sagged down. Joshua tied his horse to the hitching rail farther along. Joshua looked impeccable as always, though his nose twitched like he'd stepped in manure. Kit looked tired and dirty, with dark circles under her eyes. She was dressed as a man, though her growing hair, still too short to pull back, floated around her head with gentle curls that were rather becoming. She kept her bangs to hide a scar along her hairline.

"What's going on?" Bertha asked. Henry stood beside her, resting a bag of flour on the wagon tongue while he awaited the answer.

"About forty head are missing," said Kit.

Bertha felt, rather than saw, the tension that tightened up in Henry; he was so close.

"Did they wander off?" Bertha asked.

Kit shrugged. Henry's jaw was so tight, Bertha could see his pulse. She put her hand to her chest as she realized what this could mean for Henry's future—and her own future.

Henry looked at Bertha.

He didn't say anything, but from the strain around his eyes and his compressed lips...and just *something*... she knew what he was thinking. "Were they stolen?"

He paused a moment before answering, glancing over the foothills that led up to the mountains that already had snow capping them. "Could be." He hoisted the bag of flour and swung it over his shoulder. "How long?" Henry called over his load as he entered the house to drop the bag inside.

When he stepped back out, Kit said, "Charlie realized it late yesterday morn. We searched all day yesterday and all morning today. I'm only here because I saw you when I was up on that ridge"—she pointed in the distance—"and wanted to tell you."

Bertha turned to Joshua. "Were you searching too?"

Joshua looked startled. "What, me? No, I just arrived from town. I came to make sure you returned safely."

Over his shoulder, Bertha saw Henry shoot a look of derision at Joshua before turning to untie the horses. "I'll unhitch the horses. Kit, is Nugget nearby?"

"He's been using those cottonwoods yonder for a windbreak. I'll collect him while you unhitch." She mounted, spun her horse around and began trotting toward the creek.

Joshua stepped forward, reaching out to touch Bertha's cheek for a brief moment. "You look tired. Go inside and rest by the fire. Alsobrook will find the cattle."

She found herself startled by the intimacy and slightly embarrassed. She ought to be pleased that he cared, but she didn't feel right about it in front of Henry. Now, when did she care what other people thought? But Henry was just as tired as she was, and Kit perhaps more so.

She also felt annoyed at Joshua, who didn't seem to notice there was no smoke seeping from the chimney or that the chimney was, in fact, still unfinished. Even the fire ring, a mere ten feet from where they stood, held nothing but gray ashes.

She looked at Henry, who had the reins gathered in his hands and was just letting free the brake, purposely avoiding looking at her.

Bertha felt her face warm, and she wasn't even sure if it was embarrassment or anger. Joshua might have come out to the homestead because of her, but he still ought to help out for something so important. Ought to be neighborly, at the very least.

Well, these were her cattle, too, and she wasn't going to let some low-down scoundrels steal them. "I am going to help look too."

Henry finally looked at her, shaking his head.

"You stay. You can relay messages if any of us return with news." Before she could object, he added, "We don't have a fresh mount for you. These two need rest."

Bertha looked from Henry's two tired horses that had pulled the wagon for the past three days to Joshua's fresh horse, standing there with its head held high and ears perked forward as it looked around.

She put her hand on Joshua's horse's shoulder. She gave him a pat as she said, "Joshua, I'd like to borrow your horse."

A flash of annoyance passed over Joshua's face. He shook his head. "My dear, you must rest after your long journey. I will help Henry round up his wandering herd." He said the right words, the ones that indicated he wanted to take care of Bertha, that she had someone looking out for her finally, but with his teeth clenched…well, she'd forced him into it, and he didn't like it.

Well, she didn't like it either. "The cattle…" she bit out, but then stopped. No point in arguing when she didn't have a mount to ride. She walked over to Henry and took the reins from his hands. "I'll take care of these two."

Henry looked at her intently for a moment. Then, with a brief nod, he stepped back. "Leave the wagon here. I'll unload it tomorrow."

Just then, Kit rode up with Henry's horse, Nugget, in tow, already tacked. Henry and Joshua mounted their horses, and all three turned to ride east farther into the foothills.

Bertha watched Henry, Joshua, and Kit ride off. First, Henry: travel-weary, dusty, and worried, but his back still straight. Henry's head turned as he scanned the horizon, dipped as he checked the ground for tracks. The next, Joshua, wearing fresh town clothes, was turned toward Henry. He gestured with his hands. Bertha wished she knew what he was saying. The third, Kit, she could tell was listening intently, looking between the two men to assess them. Kit, from many years of keeping to herself, was a good listener.

Bertha knew that Kit would tell her what was discussed. She also knew that Kit was impressed with Joshua's Eastern ways and prone to look favorably toward him.

Bertha unhooked the two horses from the wagon and began to lead them around to the barn.

She was conflicted. She was used to her independence and making her own decisions. But here she was, living on one man's homestead while planning to marry the other. She resented both men for making her stay home when her cattle—her investment—were in danger. When she'd been on her own, well, no one could stop her from doing what she thought best for her business and her girls.

Suddenly, Joshua raced his horse around the corner of the cabin. He came straight to Bertha, pulling his horse to a stop in a cloud of dust. He reached one hand out, and so she placed hers in it.

"Darling Bertha. I'm sorry to leave you like this. I'll round up the cattle with Henry…and given the time, it'll likely be too late to go back to town tonight. I know you're worried about the cattle and what it means for your future. Our future. I have some ideas about that. I'll tell you in the morning." He gently pulled her toward him.

She resisted for a moment. But then she allowed herself to step closer.

Joshua leaned down from the saddle to press his lips to the

back of her hand. He winked and released her hand. He backed his horse away a few paces before spinning around again, this time to race back to Henry.

His behavior was gallant: ardent yet respectful. She should revel in it, but instead she felt she was acting in a play.

Ideas about what? Did Joshua mean ideas about the cattle? Or ideas about their future? Bertha stood there, bemused. They used to talk about business opportunities when he visited Virginia City. She relished how he told her his ideas and plans and even seemed to appreciate her insight on local issues. She'd even thought about him as a business partner and thought he might think of her the same. But now, as he was courting her, she was being seen as less capable as she changed from businesswoman to future wife.

Life didn't let you have everything you wanted, though. Bertha knew that. A person was lucky to get even a sliver of their dreams.

She thought of the nice folks at the ranch two nights before. She'd appreciated how kind and respectful they were to her. It sure would be nice if everyone treated her that way. She also noticed how hardworking the couple was—the boys too—and how Milo and Dorothea seemed a good team. An image of herself and Henry working side by side flashed in her mind.

But she wondered if the Hisers would have welcomed her into their home if they knew the truth about her. And she'd have to wonder that, always, if she stayed in Montana Territory. Her past would always be a specter ready to haunt her.

Back in the States, if she and Joshua married, she could be the woman her parents had raised her to be. She would lose her independence and her role as a businesswoman. Yet these were things she never would have known if her life had gone according to plan. Getting away from her past, getting a life of ease…it was worth the trade, wasn't it?

Bertha unbuckled and pulled the harnesses from the horses

and set them to graze. She stomped back around the cabin to start a fire and rustle up some supper. Her life of ease couldn't start just yet.

CHAPTER 12

"Kit, you head up along the creek. Hopefully, you'll run into Charlie that way. Reynolds, you cross there and head along south until you get to the edge of the canyon. If you haven't seen sign of the cattle by then, turn east a ways and then head back north. I'll head north and circle around from that direction. We'll all end up meeting up there," Henry said, pointing up the mountain to a meadow peeking out between the lodgepole pines.

"Maybe we should head right up there. Overlook the valley, and we'll spot them," said Joshua, as relaxed and unurgent as if he was talking about the style of his coat.

Henry gritted his teeth. "It's not a smooth meadow you're looking down on, Reynolds. There's ridges and dips and trees and crevices. You're looking for prints on the ground right now. You get that?"

Joshua glared at him, nodded curtly, and headed south across the creek. Kit looked from Joshua to Henry, but when Henry said nothing further, she nodded and headed up the creek.

Henry tugged on Nugget's reins. They headed uphill, away

from the cottonwoods lining the creek into the drier sagebrush country.

What Henry really wanted to do, besides find the missing cattle, was send Joshua Reynolds packing.

He was astonished that a man could succeed in Montana Territory, as Joshua seemed to be doing, when he worked so little, helped so little, and talked so much. The entire ride from the cabin, which the man undertook only because Bertha shamed him into it, he didn't stop talking about what Henry should do with the cattle and the ranch, what was best for Bozeman, and worst of all, what was best for Bertha.

Henry admitted to himself that he was strangely bothered by Joshua. He had no claim and no right, but he just didn't like the man courting Bertha. Didn't like seeing Joshua act all proprietary about Bertha. He didn't even like how proprietary he was about the cattle, as if they were his by extension of his interest in Bertha.

But today, he and Bertha needed all the help they could get so they didn't lose their investment. With any luck, one of them would run into the cows and steers soon.

Henry paused at the top of the hill. From there, he could see down the other side but also the tops of other nearby hills. The sun was heading toward setting, and the shadows were lengthening, making it easier to miss any signs of the cattle. He sighed and then pushed on.

There was something about Joshua. He was the kind of fellow ready to take advantage of the West, but not one to improve it or create his own opportunity. The kind of guy who'd buy out someone else's mining claim when that man just needed a loan to get him through a bit longer.

But, on the other hand, Joshua wanted to take care of Bertha, and a woman like her deserved it.

Henry knew how Bertha had helped the women she worked with, giving them a way to survive when they needed it, but then also helping guide the ones who wanted out of service— that kind of service, anyway. She looked out for those around her, especially those in need: like that widow woman she'd sent to the church in Virginia City, and her kindness to that Welshman. Bertha deserved a break. Henry knew lots of folks looked down on what she'd done, and frankly he was surprised Joshua wasn't one of them.

Henry wished for a moment that he could offer Bertha a life of ease like Joshua could. He knew he could be a decent husband. He'd support her and all that. Bertha would be a great wife on the ranch. She knew how to do so much and was smart enough to figure out the rest. And golly, but he'd be happy to look at her for the rest of his life. But she didn't want to work a ranch. She deserved better.

He thought of his stepmom. She was nice enough and loving to his father, but she cared only for her domain. She kept a neat house but wasn't interested in the rest of the family, or even the neighbors. Bertha, in comparison, had such a big heart, caring for everyone she came in contact with.

His thoughts returned to the present when he heard cows lowing in the distance. A wave of relief flowed through him. He tapped his heels to the horse's sides, but his mount was already speeding up. A good cow horse knew its job, Henry thought.

They walked down the steep hill, kicking up stones that cascaded down ahead of them. Tall bushes and evening shadows obscured the cows, but Henry could hear the missing cattle. It looked like they'd found a nice little seep, protected from the wind with thick dried grasses left over from the summer to eat. It seemed about perfect, except Henry wondered how they wandered in here. It looked like they'd come over the hill from the west, but it was steep enough he thought they must have had a bee in their bonnets to make it this far. But, after circling the herd, he saw no evidence of cattle rustlers or Indians or even wolves.

Henry and Nugget wove their way between the bushes and the animals until Henry had counted forty cows and steers. Knowing the cattle were unlikely to travel heading into evening, he left to climb up the ridge, zigzagging along it until he reached the meeting place. He saw Kit and Charlie and Joshua approaching and waved them over. The waning gibbous moon glowed. While he waited, he looked over the valley, surrounded by dark mountains rising up. The stars were emerging so quickly it was like watching raindrops fall up and hit the night sky.

Kit and Charlie were visibly relieved to find the herd intact. Joshua looked relieved that they could return home.

Charlie and Kit offered to stay the night with the cattle.

"They're not going anywhere tonight."

"We can round 'em up early and have 'em back before breakfast if we stay up here," said Charlie. "I'll build a fire to keep warm."

Henry hesitated, looking at Kit.

She huffed. "You wouldn't have thought twice when you still thought I was a man."

Joshua smirked at Henry.

Henry pulled out his gun.

Joshua sucked in his breath.

Henry held out his gun to Kit. "You were never a man. You were a boy. Now, take this. In case you have any trouble." He couldn't help but be amused when Joshua let out his breath in a huge gush.

Kit and Charlie headed back down to the seep with the cattle. Henry and Joshua rode the other way, back toward the cabin. The moon and stars were bright enough they didn't have trouble seeing their way down the trail.

Henry wanted to imagine the look of pleasure on Bertha's

face when he told her their investment was safe. He wanted to sit down with her in the warm cabin, eating a hot dinner by the fire. Instead, the only fire he could only look forward to would be outside in the cold night air, and the company would be shared by Joshua.

Henry looked over at Joshua, who was pushing his horse ahead, clearly wanting to reach Bertha first. His mood turned sour.

CHAPTER 13

Bertha drew the covers higher over her head. It was terribly cold in the cabin. Every gap in her blanket meant a draft of biting air would sneak in to chill her. Without Kit, Lily or Eugenie, and still lacking a working fireplace, there was no warmth but herself. It didn't help that she jumped up every so often to throw another log on the fire outside. The fire would only warm her front side, and at this late hour, she was tired enough to want to lie down. But by keeping the fire going, she kept it ready for the return of the others as well as keeping the stew warm.

She heard the clop of horse hooves and low voices in the direction of the barn. They were back. She slid out of bed, tucked her hair behind her ears, and covered her head with her shawl. Outside, she threw more logs on the fire, skimmed the ice off the water bucket, and gathered bowls and spoons for the stew.

Joshua emerged from darkness, rubbing his hands together against the cold.

"Bertha! Look at you. Playing at being the pioneer wife, are you?" He laughed as he crouched down at the fire and held his hands out. His eyes roamed the shawl wrapped over her head and shoulders. "I expect we'll both be glad to see the last of this life."

Before she could respond, Henry stepped up to the fire, also holding out his hands to warm them. From the tightness around his eyes, she feared the worst.

"Did you find them?"

Henry's face eased slightly. "We did."

She felt a wave of relief.

Joshua looked up. "They're fine. We could have waited until morning and saved ourselves the trouble, I'd say."

A muscle twitched in Henry's jaw. "We couldn't know they were fine until we found them."

Trying to avert an argument, Bertha grabbed two bowls and spooned in the stew. She handed them each one. "Where were they? Where are Kit and Charlie?"

Henry paused with his spoon midair. "In a seep a bit farther north. Kit and Charlie are there and will ride the cattle back to the herd in the morning."

Bertha nodded.

Joshua looked at Bertha. "You're not worried about Kit?" She noticed he tried to avoid saying he or she, always using Kit's name.

"Kit can take of herself. It's colder than a witch's—" She saw a look of disapproval descend over Joshua's face. "Nose, but I'm sure between Charlie and her, they can figure out how to build a fire." She heard a snort and looked at Henry, but he was studiously focused on his bowl of stew.

"I'm talking about a man and a…a woman, alone together at night. Especially one with Kit's background. Could lead to trouble." Joshua stood and held his bowl out to Bertha for seconds.

She stared at him until his hand dropped. She was aware of Henry grinning on the other side of the fire, but she ignored him. She drew her shoulders back, the fire of anger suddenly warming her.

"Her background? Do you mean because she grew up in a brothel? Because she was tainted?"

"Now, that's not what I—"

"So, do you suppose she'll fling her skirts up on this bitterly cold night? Unable to contain herself under the light of the moon?"

"Now Bertha—" Joshua entreated.

Her voice didn't rise but turned deadly angry. She tipped her head toward Henry who watched the argument with enough pleasure that she glared at him too. "What about me, Joshua? Do you suppose I am similarly tainted? Unable to be trusted alone with a man? With Henry or Charlie? Is that why you keep coming out here? Not to visit with me but to keep an eye on me?"

"You don't mean that, Bertha. You're just tired and overworked."

She put her hands on her hips.

"He gave her a gun!" Joshua pointed at Henry.

Henry, helping himself to a second bowl of stew, shrugged. "I did. Charlie's a good fellow, but you never know who's roaming the foothills. We still don't know what—or who— sent the herd a-wandering."

That was all he said, but there was a world of information in that statement. Henry's concern for Kit, yes, but also his confidence that she could defend herself if need be.

Bertha and Henry met eyes. She felt his acknowledgement of her anger.

She felt his concern for how she, Bertha, was feeling.

She felt his admiration.

Bertha felt a thrill run down her spine. What was happening? She pulled her eyes away, for once not ready with an amusing jest, and realized Joshua was watching them, his own eyes narrowed.

Joshua forced a smile and walked around the fire ring to Bertha. He held out his hands. "It's late, and it's cold. You've done enough. I'll walk you to your door, and you can finally get some sleep."

Bertha allowed herself to be led away, even if it was barely more than ten feet. She didn't know what her feelings were for either man at this moment, and she just wanted to be alone.

Joshua murmured in her ear. "You deserve better than staying up all night taking care of a couple louts like us. You deserve servants who will cook *you* dinner. In your own home with a fireplace in every room. And maybe a pretty nightcap to wear at night instead of a woolen shawl." He gently tugged the shawl until it slid from her head, pooling around her shoulders. She felt her curls springing up on her head.

Joshua stepped closer.

Bertha felt mixed emotions. Flattered that Joshua wanted to take care of her. And yet she knew he was manipulating her to distract her from their argument. She'd done it many a time in her brothel, distracting and calming angry men looking for a fight. Flattery was winning until she saw Joshua glance toward the fire, toward Henry, with a hint of a smile tugging at his lips. He was trying to prove something—prove that Bertha was his.

Bertha withdrew her hand.

"Good night, Joshua. Good night, Henry."

She entered the cabin and closed the door behind her. A small part of her appreciated Joshua's intent in claiming her. It reminded her of a barn dance when she was fourteen, before typhoid had swept through the little town, and her world had been turned upside down. Three boys had solicited her hand for dances, elbowing each other out of the way at the end of every set, each wanting to claim the next dance. She'd been young and silly, not even understanding the game they were all playing.

But it was no game this time. She'd felt the steely gaze of Henry burning into her, knew he didn't like Joshua taking her hands or whispering in her ear. She'd felt his hot gaze meet hers, and when it did, she wasn't thinking about an easy life back east, but about this strong, handsome man working his ranch under the majestic mountains. A man who didn't care about her past, only her, here and now.

Bertha leaned back on the door, letting the cold air wash over her.

CHAPTER 14

Henry and Nugget picked their way along the ridge. The mountains loomed on their right while the valley opened up on their left. The bright sun and blue sky accompanied the crisp November air. The golds and occasional reds of the early fall had faded into browns.

Henry's hunting rifle was in the saddle scabbard while he wore a pack basket on his back. He was looking for meat, but he was also surveying his land and the land nearby. He'd heard wolves howling in the distance last night. He'd also heard there was a new neighbor a little farther up the foothills: a gunrunner who had supplied both the Union and the Confederacy during the War Between the States, who was not interested in getting to know the locals. Henry didn't care if the man wanted to hole up there, but he wanted to make sure the fellow wasn't poaching Henry's cattle.

He noted a deer rub on a pine sapling. He looked for tracks, likely a young buck in the area.

Poaching. That was how he felt about Joshua. He felt like Joshua was poaching on Bertha. Yet Joshua was courting her, and Henry wasn't.

And maybe that was the problem. These past few weeks watching Joshua court Bertha hadn't sat right with Henry, even though Henry hadn't staked any claim of his own.

Henry had an idea in his head. A dream. A ranch, a wife, children. A family. He had the ranch, and he was damn proud of it. Beautiful land. It wasn't easy country, but it was worth it.

That nameless, faceless wife he'd imagined…well, Bertha's name and face kept imposing themselves on that dream image. She was beautiful. Everyone could see that. But she was also hardworking and smart. And kind. The way she looked out for those that needed looking out for. The world needed more folks like her. She'd make a damn fine ranch wife. Someone to work side by side with, sure, but also someone to talk with, laugh with, bed with.

They likely wouldn't have children. When she told them about Kit, the way she'd said, "I can't," and the bleak look in her eyes…Henry felt a small pang. He was disappointed, he admitted to himself, but truth was, children from some other wife—that wasn't what he wanted.

She had a lot of history. There were people who were going to judge her. She was strong-willed and independent. Life with her wouldn't be easy. But like the land around him, she was worth it.

Henry saw a movement on the hillside up ahead. It was the buck. He slipped off Nugget and tied him to a bush. He took his rifle out and slowly, quietly, walked toward his prey.

Bertha was worth the trouble to Henry, but was the trouble worth it to Bertha? Why would she choose to stay here in harsh Montana Territory when she could have a life of ease back in the States? Maybe her life would be better with Joshua.

He knelt on one knee, settling his rifle and sighting the buck.

Maybe Henry wasn't the one to decide for Bertha. He admired her independence and the way life didn't push her around. So, maybe he needed to pursue her and let her make her own choices.

He felt like a shadow lifted off him. He knew what he wanted and hoped Bertha wanted the same. Now, it was time to make it happen.

He pulled the trigger.

CHAPTER 15

Bertha pulled back on the reins to halt the horses. There were a few folks in the street, several of whom had stepped out of doorways when they'd heard the jangle of the harness and the creak of the wagon. Bozeman was growing, but visitors were still worth a look.

She pulled the brake on the wagon as Kit jumped off the buckboard seat. In her rush, Kit forgot she was wearing a skirt and stumbled, her legs tangling in the striped cotton fabric. The skirt and blouse had been remade from one of Bertha's outfits.

"Oh, Kit!"

Bertha watched as Kit collected herself. The young woman smoothed the fabric of her skirt, her face glowing red. She stomped over to the heads of the horses. Once she'd tied them to the hitching post, Bertha gathered her own skirts and gracefully—carefully—climbed down.

They had both, Bertha and Kit, each in their own way, spent years highly aware of all eyes on them. For Bertha, it was a combination of vigilance and advertising. Vigilance, because she was a young woman on her own in a territory full of men.

Advertising, once she'd been forced to make her own living. She hadn't wanted to do what she did, but if she was going to do it, she wanted to be treated as best she could arrange it.

For Kit, she'd had to act the boy for so long it was a challenge for her to be the young woman.

And now, Bertha was advertising again. But this time, she was doing her best to be a respectable homesteader. She had dressed carefully to come to town. She wore a dress of a nice cotton stripe with floral sprays patterned throughout, something she had reworked from a fancy gown. She'd removed some furbelows and filled in the neckline with lace she'd pulled from another gown. She'd expected to have to let out the bodice, now that she refused to wear her corset so tight, but it seemed she was working hard enough to have lost a little weight.

She didn't mind it. She still had plenty of curves, she thought with satisfaction, but they weren't quite so blatant as before. Though that might have been the corset and choice of wardrobe. She certainly didn't want to look like one of those scrawny, starving women coming over the pass, already hollow-eyed before they'd even landed at their destination. There were only a few wagon trains still straggling across the pass at this time of year, and they all looked the worse for wear.

Bertha and Kit stepped across the boardwalk. Kit chose to stay outside and watch the horses, not that they were going anywhere. Bertha entered the mercantile and introduced herself to the shopkeeper.

"I heard you were out there on Alsobrook's ranch." He nodded politely but didn't offer to shake her hand. Bertha detected the question in his eyes. *You seem respectable, but I've heard about your previous life in Virginia City. Have you really turned over a new leaf?* He pursed his lips.

There were more people than just herself trying to reinvent

themselves in Montana Territory. Most came a lot farther, so their pasts were more hidden. But little escaped notice.

She handed her list to the shopkeeper. He reviewed it, asked for a bit of clarification, and told her he'd get her packages and load them on her wagon out front.

"Have you any mail for myself, Henry, Kit, or Charlie?" Henry had told her that mail was delivered there since the town didn't yet have a post office.

"Well now, let's see. I believe I do." He walked over to the far end of the counter and pulled out a small box. His fingers flicked rapidly through the small envelopes, pulling out three which he laid on the counter while he put the box away. He carried the three back to Bertha. "Here's one for you. This here one is for Alsobrook. And it's not Kit, but there is one here for Catherine O'Malley. Do you know her?"

Bertha's breath caught.

No one knew Kit's real name, not since she'd started dressing as a boy back in California Territory. When they'd moved out to Alsobrook's ranch, they'd discussed calling her Catherine again, but just acknowledging she was a young woman had been enough of a change. Bertha hadn't wanted to force it.

"Yes, I'll take it. She's right outside." He handed her the letter. The address was written in an elegant, masculine hand. The paper quality was good. It looked as though it had been forwarded from Virginia City, where it had sat, from the postmark, for quite a while before making its way to Bozeman.

The postmark was from Chicago. From where Kit's mother had originally emigrated.

Bertha wanted to rip it open.

She wanted to burn it, never to be read.

Kit had been her charge—her daughter—for nearly seven years. What good could come from this surprise from the past?

Bertha slipped the three letters into her pocket.

She finished her shopping, left the merchant to fill her order, and stepped outside. Kit was pacing back and forth along the boardwalk, her long skirts swishing each time she spun around. Her eyes surveyed all with a directness less common in a young woman.

"Are we under attack?" Bertha asked.

Kit stopped abruptly. "No." She smiled. "But only because I've been keeping lookout." Bertha loved how the girl could laugh at herself. She decided to hold the letter for the return trip home. She didn't know what it said, but she suspected some privacy would be in order.

"Come," Bertha said, "Joshua will be waiting for us at the hotel."

Joshua had visited Bertha at the ranch a number of times, always commenting on the amount of work she had to do while living out there. Today, at least, she could enjoy their visit without having to work. It would be a pleasure to eat food cooked by someone else and to know she would not have to wash or even oversee the cleaning up. She hadn't lived the high life in Virginia City, but she had occasionally enjoyed some of the benefits of living in town. She missed it at times.

Bertha and Kit left the horses tied to the hitching post. Bertha tossed a coin to the merchant's young son. "Keep an eye on them, will you?"

He nodded eagerly.

The two women headed to the hotel. Joshua had had a basket of food brought over from the only restaurant in town. They sat in the semi-private room off the lobby. Joshua held out Bertha's chair with a flourish. He reached out to a chair for Kit, but she slid into one on the opposite side of the table. Joshua looked annoyed as he sat down but tried to cover it up.

Bertha lifted her fork to her mouth and carefully chewed. She felt oddly on display. Joshua's hungry eyes had no interest in the food; he couldn't take his eyes off her. In the past, she had often enjoyed the attention of the males around her. But there was a difference between admiration and lust, and today…well, in either case, it felt inappropriate with Kit right there. Joshua was completely ignoring Kit, to the point of rudeness, but it didn't particularly matter because Kit wasn't paying him any attention either.

She was also staring at Bertha, but for a completely different reason. After so many years dressing and acting like a boy, Kit's feminine table manners were lacking. She was self-conscious enough in a dress, but add in manners, and Kit was rather uncertain. So she was copying Bertha's every move. When Bertha cut her meat, Kit cut her meat. When Bertha raised her fork to her mouth, Kit raised her fork to her own mouth.

Bertha wanted to laugh, but she knew neither of her dining companions would see the humor in the awkward dinner. Regardless of the reason, with Joshua on the one side and Kit on the other, there was little conversation.

Bertha put down her fork and reached for her coffee, wishing it was something stronger. She heard the clatter of a fork and saw Kit had dropped hers on her plate and was lunging for her own cup. The cup tipped and spilled coffee across the tablecloth.

Joshua pushed away from the table, cussing. Kit turned beet red. She scrambled to blot up the brown stain between the plates.

"It's just coffee," said Bertha, arching one eyebrow.

Joshua brushed at his pants uselessly. "I don't know that I should have expected anything more than this, given where the girl was raised."

Kit froze.

Bertha leaned over, placing one hand on Kit's forearm to get her to sit back.

Joshua didn't look up as he fumed. "Dressing as a boy,

surrounded by whores. Now she's riding the range like a cowboy. It's a wonder she doesn't burn up in flames just wearing a dress."

Bertha felt a tide of anger wash over her. She was used to being insulted. Maybe not by Joshua, but somehow it seemed inevitable. But Kit. Kit was her daughter to protect, in her heart, if not by birth.

Slowly Bertha rose. She smoothed her skirts, aware in the back of her mind that she wished she had her full Big Bertha regalia on. It had felt like armor in a way that this pioneer dress, even a go-to-town dress, didn't.

Joshua looked up and met Bertha's steely gaze. She saw the dawning of his awareness of her anger. He jumped to his feet.

"I—"

Bertha held up her hand. "How dare you."

"Well, I—" he blustered.

"No. You have insulted me. And you have insulted Kit."

Kit, still sitting, swiveled back and forth between the two speakers.

"I am sorry, Bertha. I didn't mean to insult you in any way."

"That's ridiculous. I am her mother, and you insulted us both."

Joshua threw a scornful look at Kit. "You are not her mother."

"I am." Bertha reached over and took Kit's hand. "Of course I am."

Kit stood up beside Bertha. Her eyes were a mix of anger, hurt, and pride. Bertha squeezed her hand gently before turning back to Joshua. She raised both eyebrows, waiting.

After a moment, he realized Bertha wasn't going to let it be. He offered an exaggerated bow. "Please forgive me, my ladies."

The insincerity was like a slap in Bertha's face. She stepped back, Kit staying right at her side.

"We're leaving."

Joshua shoved the chair back and stomped toward them. "You can't walk out on me."

Bertha paused, straightening her shoulders. "In fact, I can. For now, at least, I can."

At that, Joshua stopped. They were not married, not yet, and he had no claims on Bertha. Hesitation skittered across his face. He pulled on his waistcoat, for want of something to do with his hands, white knuckles glaring.

Bertha put her arm through Kit's. Together, they walked out the door, through the lobby and out onto the sunny boardwalk.

A swirl of emotions buffeted her inside, but Bertha knew her outside was calm as could be. She had perfected that trait many years ago. She pulled Kit in closer for the briefest moment but kept walking.

Kit's lips pressed together, a sure sign she had a lot to say and was struggling to hold it back.

"Not yet," Bertha said under her breath. She nodded to the cooper, taking a break outside his shed. She smiled at Rumor, the barkeep from the only other hotel bar in town, who was sweeping the boardwalk in front of his bar.

How could Bertha have a respectable future if even Joshua, a man who claimed to care for her, claimed to respect her, couldn't forget her past? He talked about Kit, but what he meant was *Bertha's* past.

They walked back to the mercantile. After reviewing the purchases, they checked the harnesses and prepared to leave.

"You'd better let me drive," said Bertha, reaching into her pocket. "You have a letter to read."

Bertha handed the letter to Kit and took up the reins. She didn't know who sent the letter, or why, and she was afraid.

Henry paused in the doorway to watch Bertha.

She stood at the table, her hands deep in dough. She knew how to cook and wasn't half bad, except when it came to baking. She was as likely to scorch the bread as leave it wet and undercooked inside. Henry admired her determination to master whatever task she set her mind to, though he hoped she'd master this task sooner rather than later.

Likely it would be later, because at the moment, she wasn't actually doing anything to the bread. Her head was down, her shoulders slumped, and her hands were still. She hadn't noticed Henry enter the open door of the cabin. Of course, with a dirt floor there were no boards to creak.

"From the amount of flour on your apron, I'd guess you had to rassle that bread dough before it submitted."

Bertha jerked from surprise. She looked up. Her face was dusted with flour, too, which would have been sweet except for the tear tracks running through it.

Henry reached over and began to gently brush the flour, and tracks, from Bertha's face. She closed her eyes and leaned ever so slightly into his hand. Another tear hovered in her eyelashes.

"Bertha?"

Her eyes, more blue than gray at the moment, opened, shining with wet. A deep sadness etched itself across her face. She opened her mouth to speak, but her voice caught.

Henry reached forward and gently pulled her hands from the dough. He used her apron to brush the flour and bits of sticky dough from her hands.

She allowed him to treat her so gently, but after a moment, she squared her shoulders and tried to push his hands away. "I've got to knead this bread, or it won't be good."

Henry put his arm across her shoulders and began to steer her toward the doorway. "It's rarely good, so it makes no matter."

Bertha gasped as Henry maneuvered her outside to the bench. They sat side by side. The November wind carried away much of the sun's warmth. Dreary gray clouds hung low.

Henry left his arm around Bertha, pulling her in close. "What's got you blue-devilled?"

Bertha turned her head to look at him. Henry could feel the pain radiating out of her. This strong woman who had weathered everything with such aplomb had finally been brought low. He wondered what had happened in town yesterday. She'd been quiet at dinner last night and again this morning. He'd thought maybe she didn't want to return to the ranch life, that she'd been wishing she could stay in town with Joshua, but now he wasn't so sure.

"Bertha?"

"We picked up a letter at the post office yesterday. A letter to Kit."

Henry waited while Bertha twisted her apron back and forth.

"Kit's mother wrote to her family from California when she

found out she was to have a child, but they never wrote back. She had run away with a young man they didn't approve of. When she died—and the father, too—I took in the baby. She was called Cathy, and I kept her safe as could be; I did. I even had her start dressing as a boy so she'd be safe from the men, like I told you already. Despite where she was raised, she never had to work."

It was left unsaid. Work as a whore.

"You don't have to convince me, Bertha. She's a capable young woman who clearly loves you like a mother."

Bertha squeezed her eyes tight. She opened them and grabbed Henry's hand. "I love her like a daughter. She *is* my daughter. The only one I've ever had."

"The letter?"

"The letter was from her family—her true mother's family —back in Chicago. Her grandparents died, and a son, Kit's uncle, found the letter about her in a box. He's been searching for her and has invited her to return to Chicago—home, as he wrote—and live a life of affluence and even go to girls' school."

"She doesn't even know this fellow," said Henry. "You don't know if he's telling the truth. She can't just travel across the country alone and show up at his door and hope for the best."

Bertha slowly nodded. "I don't know anything about the mother, except that she came from money. She left a lovely sapphire pendant that I've held for Kit all these years. I gave it to her this morning." She sighed. "The uncle says to write to him, and he'll arrange for her safe travel. Apparently, he has mining interests in Last Chance Gulch. He mentions his agent whom she can depend on. I know of the man. He has a good reputation, and the mine has paid out well."

"That doesn't mean Kit has to go."

"Oh, Henry. How can I discourage her? She can go live her life without having to haul water, chase cows all night or bake this stupid bread! No one will question where she was raised or why she dressed as a boy for so many years." She pulled back from him. He let his arm drop. "She can have the companionship of other women, not just an ex-whore and a bunch of cowhands. If she stays here, she'll end up marrying some homesteader with a sod cabin that drops voles from the ceiling every time it rains."

Henry felt like his own heart had been ripped out. He'd only just begun to imagine Bertha staying, making a life with her. A life he'd dreamed of for years. But if this was how Bertha felt about it for Kit, then surely she felt the same for herself.

The wind pushed clouds in front of the sun, making the bite of the wind that much worse.

"So, she wants to go?"

Bertha gave a half laugh. "Not particularly. But I told her she needed to write back. It's an opportunity like she'll never have if she stays here."

Henry felt like he'd never understand the workings of a female mind. "If she doesn't want to and it makes you so sad, then why are you pushing this?"

"Oh, Henry. She's too young to know better. She doesn't know any life but the hard one. I know the hard one, Henry." Her voice turned hard too. "I know it, and I want better for her. No one will ever let her forget Kit here, even if she wants to be Cathy. She deserves it."

Bertha deserved it too. Henry looked out at his land. What had seemed so promising when he'd entered the cabin, golden grasses to support his cattle—his dreams—now looked brown and dead, soon to be pinned to the ground by the snow of the long, bleak winter ahead. He'd been thinking of trying to convince Bertha to stay, to marry him and not that damned Joshua. But she deserved an easier life. She'd had a hard one long enough.

Henry placed his free hand over Bertha's, which still

gripped his other hand tightly, and squeezed gently. "You know, Bertha, it won't be so hard for you to visit Kit from St. Louis. You won't see her so often, but travel between those two cities is regular."

A mixture of hope and confusion flashed across her face.

Henry slowly extracted his hands from Bertha's and stood. "Now, you best get back inside. That bread won't knead itself, though it'd probably taste better if it did."

Bertha gave a laugh-sob and lightly slapped him on the arm.

"Henry, I—"

"It's alright, Bertha. Now, I've got some tools to sharpen."

She looked at him for a moment, nodded, and turned to enter the cabin.

Henry shivered as the wind crawled under his shirt. Felt like some bad weather was headed their way.

CHAPTER 17

The wind whipped the clothes on the line. Each piece removed had to be held tightly so it didn't fly away. Kit brought the pieces, one by one, to Bertha, who had set up the ironing board outside. She alternated irons, letting each in turn heat itself at the small fire she had built in the fire pit. The wind whipped the flames, too, so she moved a water bucket to help block it.

"Bertha, why do you keep on about going to school back East? I can read and write and do my numbers." Kit handed Bertha a stack of handkerchiefs.

"Kit, you've got family."

"Family I never knew. You're my family."

"Kit." Bertha paused her iron and took a deep breath. "If you stay here, you'll never have any options. You'll marry a miner or a rancher or a shopkeeper."

"Is that so bad?"

Bertha tucked her hair back.

"Look. Everyone knows you here. The girl who grew up in a bordello and dressed like a boy. You're never going to get the respect you deserve. It's not easy to live a life where people cross to the other side of the road to avoid contact with you. Whisper behind their hands at you. To know they're looking down on you when they have no right to do so. Kit, I did what I had to do to survive. But it's not a life I'd have chosen, if I had a choice. *You* have a choice."

Kit grumbled. "Everyone else is heading West, and I'm heading East."

Bertha reached for a fresh iron and nearly burnt her hand. She grabbed a rag for the iron handle.

Going East was best for them both. Even so, Bertha was fearing her own trip East. The way Joshua had treated them, how could she be sure her own history wouldn't come out? She could make a big change and still be Big Bertha to others.

Kit looked around. "How can I leave this? It's all I know."

Bertha looked up. The sky was the color of a bluebird's wing. Thin wisps of clouds contrasted with the dark mountain peaks. The foothills flowed in gold and straw colors. A red-tailed hawk glided overhead.

How could she, Bertha, leave it?

Before she could think further on the unexpected question, she heard her name called out. Riding up the path from town was Joshua. As he approached, Bertha took the cooled iron and used it to weigh down the handkerchiefs. She stepped away from the board and walked toward Joshua. She'd rather have walked the other way, but she knew it best to face the conflicts head- on. She put sass in her step and let the wind pull her blond curls free. I'll remind him of who I am, she thought.

Joshua dismounted and tied his horse to the hitching post before approaching the women. He took his hat from his head and held it between his hands. "Don't go, Miss Kit. I'd like to speak with you both."

Kit had been about to walk away, but instead she went and stood beside Bertha.

Bertha crossed her arms. Kit did the same.

"I owe you both an apology. I wasn't a gentleman."

Bertha didn't say anything.

"I hope you'll forgive me, Bertha." He tipped his head and gave her puppy dog eyes.

She uncrossed her arms. This was the charming Joshua she was used to.

"What you said was hurtful, Joshua. To both of us. I can't change my past, and Kit can't change hers. If you can't get over that…"

"I can, Bertha. I am over that." He stepped closer, his admiring eyes meeting hers. "You know that I admire you. I just imagine how others would react if they knew. In St. Louis, you'll see how well I treat you. You'll never have to stand in a cold wind doing your chores." He waved his hand toward the irons and board. "You'll have a new name, and we can both forget about Big Bertha's life."

He looked at Kit. "And you're turning into a fine young lady. I am sorry for what I said."

She nodded. "Excuse me. I'm going to take a walk." She turned and headed for the corral.

Joshua reached out and took Bertha's red, work-worn hand. He raised it and put his other hand over it, standing directly in front of her. He lifted her hand and kissed the back of it. "Your hands will be smooth and soft again when you're in your own house. I promise you. You'll have a maid to do your ironing. A cook to make your supper." His voice was nearly a whisper, drawing her in. "The neighbors will tip their hats and curtsy at the fine, upstanding woman living next door. You'll be invited to balls and teas and have pretty dresses to wear."

Oh, the life he promised. She felt the corners of her lips turning up and her heart lightening. It was going to happen. Her dreams would come true. And it would be wonderful.

CHAPTER 18

"Are you sure this is a good idea?" Henry asked.

"Of course it is," Bertha snapped.

Henry pushed his hat back and ran his fingers through his hair. He was fairly certain that Kit wished she could do the same. Bertha had the girl pinned and beribboned and wrapped up so tight she could barely move. Bertha had been schooling the girl for weeks, and they both seemed miserable.

"It's just…" He paused under Bertha's glare but pushed ahead anyway. "Kit doesn't seem like herself anymore."

A tide of red washed over Bertha's skin. If her anger had been aimed at anyone but him, he'd have been glad to sit back and enjoy the show. As it was, he tried not to be distracted by her heaving bosom as she took deep breaths.

"She's not herself, Henry," Bertha bit out. "She's not Kit. She's Catherine."

Kit looked up, her lips pressed together. "I'm—"

"Catherine. You are *Catherine*. Not a smock-faced boy anymore. And *Catherine* is a lovely young lady without a common nickname like Kit. And *Catherine* will want to be accepted as a lovely young lady when she goes to the States. *Catherine* will learn her manners and dress appropriately."

Kit's hands, which had been resting in her lap, one hand gently cupping the other, slid down to grip the side of the bench on which she was sitting, white knuckled. She closed her eyes for a moment.

Henry watched a flash of pain skip across Bertha's face. She only wanted what was best for Kit. He just wasn't sure this was it.

Kit stood up. "*Catherine* is in need of a break. *Catherine* is going to take a walk. *Alone.*" Like the proper young lady Bertha was trying to invent, she glided across the yard with perfect posture, the light breeze gently teasing her ribbons. As the meadow grass encroached on the trail, however, Kit reached down to pull up her skirts and began running as fast as she could down the path toward the creek.

Bertha whirled on Henry. "I thought you were going to help."

He took a step forward. "I'm trying to help. I walked her around the yard and asked her to dance and brought her a drink and did all those silly things you asked. *Kit* hated it. She hates having her hair all pinned up and her"—he motioned his hands up and down his sides—"all constricted with a corset."

"It's what she has to do," Bertha hissed.

"No, Bertha, it's what you want her to do. She's only doing it for you, because she'd do anything for you. But you can't change the past by forcing Kit into the life you wanted."

Bertha gasped. "How dare you—" She choked on her words.

Henry's own anger boiled out of him. "I dare because I care! You're going to force her away from everything and everyone she knows so she can go to some girls' school to learn to pour tea and embroider. Why? Because you wish someone had done that for you. But her path is different. She's had an unconventional upbringing, sure, but that's what makes her worth her weight in gold out here on the frontier. She can find a good man here, one who accepts her for who she is, and be a heck of a lot happier for it."

Bertha stared at him, still.

"And as for yourself. Do you think you're going to be any happier locked up in your St. Louis mansion with fancy-man Joshua making kissy faces at you? You need a challenge, and you need to care for others, and you need to be yourself and not pretend to be some perfect lady who's never put a toe out of line."

"That's easy for you to say, Henry. You've not been spit on and told you'll never get to heaven. You've never had a shop-keeper pretend you're not standing in front of him so he doesn't have to serve you. I don't see how you have any call to judge me for wanting to leave 'Big Bertha' behind."

Henry whacked his hat against leg, causing dust to flash out. "Dammit, Bertha. Running away isn't going to change who you are on the inside. You want a new name? What's wrong with Beebee? You're still that girl." He lowered his voice. "You're Beebee. You're Bertha. You're even Big Bertha, whether you like it or not. But you're not only her." Henry paused. Bertha stared at him, silently, tears in her eyes. He didn't like hurting her, but the words spilled out. "Just like *Catherine* will always have Kit in her."

A single tear slid down Bertha's cheek. She turned away, facing up at the mountains.

Henry spun on his heel, walking to the barn where he had tied up Nugget. He saddled the horse and headed out toward the herd. He always found it soothing to ride among the cattle, hearing the lows and quiet noises. He pushed his heels into the sides of the horse to speed him up.

"Should have kept my big mouth shut," he muttered. Maybe not about Kit. He truly believed Bertha was making a mistake pushing the girl to go off to the city with strangers. But for herself, well, Bertha was a grown woman. She knew what she wanted.

And what she didn't want.

A ranch outside of Bozeman, or anywhere in Montana Territory, seemed to be what she didn't want. Henry felt a tightening in his chest. He was feeling altogether too much for Bertha. For a woman who wanted to live a life easier than anything he could ever offer her.

Bertha was beautiful, caring and hardworking. He'd be proud to have her at his side in life. Every muscle in his body protested, but Henry had to admit to himself the truth. The life Bertha wanted was the life that Joshua could give her.

He dug his heels into Nugget's sides, and they took off at a gallop, the only sound the pounding of the horse's hooves and the dry rustling of the grasses surrounding them.

CHAPTER 19

Bertha sat in the dim light, next to the fire. Henry had completed the fireplace and chimney, for which Bertha was grateful. Cooking inside meant the wind wasn't whipping the heat away from the pots and that she wasn't shivering with cold.

A shiver ran up her spine anyway, but it wasn't from cold. She was waiting.

Waiting for Mr. and Mrs. Ronald Belkovich, agents of Catherine's uncle, to come take Catherine away.

To come take Kit away.

Bertha reached out and placed her hand over Kit's. She squeezed it gently.

Kit turned her hand over and squeezed back. "Please, Bertha…"

Bertha shook her head. "You've got to try, Kit. There's a whole other world back East. You're scared, but you won't be for long."

Kit opened her mouth to say more, but just then Henry pushed open the door and leaned his head in. "They're coming up the trail."

Bertha stood, pulling Kit up with her. It would have been easier on the Belkovichs if they'd met the couple in town, but Bertha hadn't wanted to take a chance of anyone saying anything to them about Bertha's past or Kit's upbringing.

Bertha smoothed her skirt and patted her hair. She'd worked hard to look like a decent, respectable frontier woman. She looked up and saw Kit standing there, frozen. She grabbed the girl and wrapped her arms around her, suddenly not caring about creases in her armor. Kit's arms squeezed around Bertha.

Thank goodness she'd already plied Kit with all the advice she could think of, because now she could barely speak. "I love you, Kit. You are the daughter I never had."

Kit squeezed Bertha harder.

Henry coughed from the doorway. The two women pulled apart and marched outside.

The Belkovichs drove their wagon into the yard.

Bertha waved again. She wasn't even sure if Kit was looking back to see her because the tears in her eyes blurred her vision. She gritted her teeth and forced the smile on her face to remain, suspecting it was more grimace than anything remotely pleasant. She was aware of Henry, standing by her side but a little behind her. He'd grown to admire Kit, but he had no role in her life that could be acknowledged to the couple taking Kit away. They couldn't explain how he'd been teaching her how to run cattle.

Bertha carefully, brittlely, turned and walked toward the cabin. She lurched from the doorway, realizing she couldn't bear to enter the dark cabin knowing Kit's chair and Kit's bed would remain empty. She followed the wall of the cabin around the corner. There, out of sight of the trail that would roll out toward the Missouri River and the steamboats heading back to the States, she collapsed against the logs. She wrapped her arms around her waist. Tears rushed out of her eyes, and sobs rent from her throat.

She'd sent away the only family she'd had since she was sixteen years old.

Her knees gave way, and she began to slide down. But she was caught up, suddenly, in Henry's strong arms. He pulled her into his embrace, holding her up as her body gave in to the grief. She tucked her head down and let all of the sadness cry out. Wave after wave, her face tightening until it felt like she was squeezing her eyelids inside out.

Henry held her, silently.

As her sobs slowed down and her breath stopped gasping, he began to rub circles on her shoulder blades.

She knew he disapproved of her sending Kit to her family in Chicago. He hadn't said anything else since their argument, but his eyes had told her he still didn't agree. And yet now, he comforted her.

Without looking up, still tucked in his embrace, she said, "You must think I'm crazy, sending her away and then crying like a baby."

"I know you love her, Bertha," Henry murmured into her hair.

She felt another spasm of grief, and she clutched his coat. "Like a daughter. The only daughter I'll ever have."

There was a hitch in the circles on her back. And then Henry said, "Maybe you and Joshua…"

"No," Bertha said. "We won't have children." She felt a hole inside her open up, but it was only partly because of that. Somehow, Henry talking about her future with Joshua, well, that hole kept growing bigger.

Henry pulled back, lifting her chin with his hand. "There's always kids that need a mama, just like Kit."

She shook her head. Joshua had made it clear that he

wasn't bothered at all that she couldn't have children. She rather thought he was glad.

Henry gently untangled himself from her, not letting go until he was sure she wouldn't collapse again.

"You made your choice."

Outrage stamped out the sadness inside of her. Her choice? Her choice to be abused and damaged until her body couldn't do what she wished it could? Her choice to survive any way she could? Her choice that other people couldn't tolerate that? That was why she had to leave. Even Henry couldn't forget her past as "Big Bertha."

No one could.

She pulled back, bumping into the log wall behind her. She wished she could walk away today. Walk straight into her new life in St. Louis. Maybe Joshua wasn't perfect, but at least he agreed with her dreams and was going to help her achieve them.

But before she could walk away, Henry did.

CHAPTER 20

Henry grabbed Nugget and headed out. He would check on the herd and then find Charlie, who had ridden farther up the foothills to find firewood. Swinging an axe over and over would suit Henry right now. The air was cold, and a skiff of snow covered the grasses farther up the hillside. It was a terrible time to head East. The Belkovichs and Kit, they'd be lucky to make it down the Missouri before ice set in.

He'd hated seeing Kit driving away with those strangers, even excepting the time of year. The girl tried to be brave, but he could see how miserable she was. He'd hated seeing Bertha crumple in her grief. She usually kept herself bottled up, and it was terrible to see someone so strong be so exposed.

He'd hated most of all that she was still planning to marry Joshua and go live in isolated ease. She might like it at first, but she'd get bored quickly. Sitting on a fancy settee, a cup of tea in one hand, staring at a fire while Joshua headed off to work... Bertha was a lively woman who needed challenges. Good challenges going forward, he hoped for her, but challenges still.

And she needed people. She was a helper, no doubt about it. Joshua was a damn fool not to embrace the whole of Bertha.

That was what made him so angry. She'd made her choice to marry Joshua and go live somewhere where she could only be part of herself.

Fine, thought Henry.

He heard the thwack of an axe hitting wood in the distance. He guided Nugget through the trees until he found Charlie. The young man had felled a dead tree, limbed it, and cut the log into sections that he was just starting to split.

"You've been busy," Henry said, dismounting.

Charlie put the axe down and put his hat on his sweaty head. "It helped take my mind off…"

Henry felt the anger inside of himself soften for a moment. He wasn't the only one disheartened by Kit leaving.

He nodded at Charlie. "Why don't you go check the herd and round up any strays. It'll do you good to get out of the shade and into the sun." He smiled. "Take Nugget."

A wide grin split Charlie's face. "Yes, sir!" He took the reins and mounted. "Should I come back here?"

"No," said Henry. "I'll walk back with the lumber." He gestured to Charlie's horse, which was to be used with a travois to drag the cut wood back.

Charlie lit out, and Henry picked up the axe. He swung the axe into the log. The impact jarred up into his shoulders. His pa would tell him he wasn't using his smarts right now, only his muscles. But he didn't care. The brutal smack that shook through his entire body was just what he needed. Soon, sweat dripped off his brow, despite the cold air.

He was going to forget about Bertha. As soon as she moved out. In four or five months.

Thwack!

He had to stop thinking about her future and think about his own.

Thwack!

Henry decided to pick up a newspaper next time he went to town. He'd look for an advertisement for a mail order bride.

Thwack! The log split in two. He set up one half and raised his axe.

He'd find a woman who wanted to live in Montana Territory.

Wanted to live on a ranch.

Wanted to work hard and have a good life.

Wanted to have a family—a family of some kind.

Wanted to be with Henry.

Thwack!

CHAPTER 21

Bertha sat on the bench in front of Joshua's hotel. The boardwalk and the hotel, heck, even most of the buildings in Bozeman, were still so freshly built that they hadn't weathered fully gray. The dirt street in front of her was a mix of high points, dry to the point of dust, and low points filled with half-melted snow. It was quiet. The only sound was the swish of a broom from somewhere nearby.

Bertha pulled her shawl tighter. Even in the sun, even without a breeze, the air had a bite. The mountains in the distance might look beautiful covered in snow, but they heralded the beginning of a winter that would be cold and brutal.

She had come to town with Henry. He'd left her in front of the mercantile while he headed south to a Crow Indian encampment to do some trading. She'd left her list with the merchant and walked over to wait at Joshua's.

Bertha saw in the distance a dust trail rising. She held her hand over her eyes to shade them from the sun. It was hard to tell from the distance just who was coming. She watched until she saw it was a wagon train drawing into town, coming up from Wyoming through Indian Territory, on a trail that was likely eaten bare by this time of year. They'd made it over the pass, which luckily wasn't snowed in, but just barely. These emigrants were lucky to have made it through in time.

Even a year ago, Bertha would have expected to find the wagon train full of mostly men, all headed to the gold mines. Maybe they'd be going to Virginia City. Maybe they'd head up to Last Chance Gulch, their hopes and dreams attached to a pan.

But now, there was a good chance there were homesteaders alongside the would-be miners. Folks planning to break into sod that had never seen a plow before, to farm peas or wheat or whatever they could grow in the short, hot growing season of Montana Territory. But these folks…well, what a terrible time to arrive. No time to put in a garden. They'd have to live in their wagons while they built cabins, if they could do it before a load of snow was dumped on the territory.

Bertha stood. She entered the hotel lobby.

Unlike the other hotel in town, there was no bar or kitchen for the public or tables for sitting about. It was a small, simple room that still had a hint of the smell of fresh-cut wood. There was one doorway to the stairs and another to a storage room. The third led to a larger room in the back where Joshua liked to host card games or sometimes let it for community meetings. The room where he'd hosted the lunch for her and Kit that had gone so wrong.

At the moment, he was back there with some of the town's founders and a big map of the area. They had grandiose ideas of what the town could become. They were hoping to make Bozeman the Territorial capital, if they could wrest the title from Virginia City.

The door was open, so Bertha knocked on the frame. The men looked up with looks of admiration, except from Joshua, who looked irritated.

"Bertha." He walked toward her with a smile and a sunny voice, but his jaw was clenched and his eyes daggers. They'd argued earlier when he refused to include her in the meeting. In Virginia City, for better or worse, she had been a business owner. A valued business owner in that town. She participated in a number of local community discussions. But now, she didn't count.

She retained her smile, smoothly stepping forward to place her hand in Joshua's outstretched one. He stopped at her side but held on to her hand, effectively preventing her from stepping farther into the room. She gritted her teeth.

"Joshua." She let his name drip off her tongue like honey. "I thought you gentlemen would like to know there's a wagon train approaching."

The men jumped into action. The map was rolled up. Each had a business that would likely benefit from the wagon train, whether it was the mercantile, the blacksmith, the bank, the cooper, or most certainly, the saloon. They wanted today's business, but also they needed to encourage the people to stay in Bozeman. The men dreaming of fast riches would move on to the mines, but the ones looking for land, well, why not Bozeman?

Joshua had to let go of Bertha's hand to shake the hands of the others. Bertha slipped out of the room and back outside. She'd seen the contrition in Joshua's eyes, felt the squeeze of his hand when he realized why she'd disturbed their meeting. But it still irritated her because she had indeed been a disturbance to him. When he used to take her to dinner in Virginia City, they would talk shop. He had treated her more like a man than a woman, even while he extended her the courtesies due a respectable woman.

She stood on the boardwalk, watching the wagons continue their slow approach. She had nothing to offer them. Joshua liked for her to rest prettily outside his hotel. He thought her elegant appearance would appeal to families who might want to stay in Bozeman for a night or forever.

Joshua's success was soon to be her success, but she still resented feeling so useless. She wasn't alone now, though. Everyone in town was standing in front of their businesses, awaiting the wagon train, watching the dust it churned up into the air. This was likely the last wagon train of the year. The last chance for fresh news from home. The last chance for a big payday.

Bertha wondered where Henry was. He would enjoy seeing the wagons roll into town. Not much out of the ordinary happened around here, so this was big excitement. He was supposed to pick her and the purchases up. She decided to walk over to the mercantile and make sure her order was complete. The storekeeper was sure to be plenty busy as soon as the wagons arrived. Buying or selling, lots of folks would want his attention.

By the time she finished at the store, the wagons were lined up down the center of Main Street. She paused on the board-walk, enjoying the hubbub. She missed that from Virginia City.

She walked back to Joshua's hotel. Along the way, she received several admiring glances from men, a few wishful ones from women.

When she arrived, Joshua was standing in the street, in a discussion with the wagon master. She recognized Smitty, long-time trail master, from his many visits to Virginia City. She smiled and waved.

In the distance, she watched a man with a bushy brown beard go from doorway to doorway, dragging a girl with him. It appeared they had come in with the wagon train.

The bearded man approached Bertha, his hand wrapped tightly around the arm of the girl. The scrawny girl looked to be thirteen or fourteen. She had the dirty, worn look that most emigrants had after months on the trail, but without the excited eyes that came with reaching their destination.

"Ma'am, you need a maid? A helper?"

"I do not." She didn't like this man. The hairs on the backs of her arms rose.

"Ma'am, you've got to take her. She'll be right helpful to you."

She glanced at the girl. "This is your daughter?"

"No, ma'am. Her whole family got sick and died three days past Fort Laramie. But I've got my own family and can't afford another mouth to feed. She's helpful. You'll see."

Bertha hesitated. This man had been up and down the street, and no one could afford to take on a dependent going into winter. No one would do the charitable thing. It was mostly men anyway, and taking in a young woman wasn't proper.

The man swung toward Joshua. He pushed the girl in front of him.

"Ain't there *anyplace* in town she can work? She's old enough to work."

Bertha inhaled sharply. His meaning was clear.

Bertha's blood boiled. *Any* place, he'd said with meaning. She knew if he kept the girl on till Virginia City, which was always the destination of Smitty's wagon trains, the girl would end up either in a brothel or the near-child "bride" of a miner.

Sometimes proper didn't matter.

Bertha knew the man didn't know her reputation, but she thought he likely wouldn't care, either. But if she took this girl in, well, what would become of her? She was leaving in the spring to go to St. Louis with Joshua. He certainly wouldn't like it. And she really hadn't the right to bring the girl back to Henry's ranch. And being with Bertha, well, that couldn't help the girl's reputation. Bertha might be reformed, but not everyone could forget the past. Especially someone else's past.

Joshua eyed her with a look. It was a don't-you-dare look. Then she looked back at the girl. She recognized those hollow eyes. The girl had lost her family and thought she had nothing left. But she did have something left, and Bertha was determined to make sure the girl didn't lose what was left of her childhood innocence.

"What's your name?"

"Hope, ma'am."

Hope? Oh, the irony.

"Can you dig potatoes? Haul water? Can't say I like those tasks."

The girl nodded slightly.

"I'll take her."

The man looked relieved. The girl's eyes flashed up at Bertha but quickly returned to staring at the boardwalk beneath their feet.

Joshua stepped to her side and gripped her arm. He bit out under his breath, "What are you doing?"

Bertha looked him in the eye. "I know what I am doing. Do you know what you are doing?" She glanced down at his hand wrapped around her arm. He loosened his grip, spun around and stomped off.

"Get your stuff, Hope," she said to the girl. "Meet me over at the livery." She pointed down the street. She wasn't going to wait any longer here.

Hope shook the man's hand off her arm and headed back down the line of wagons. Bertha walked parallel to her, staying on the boardwalk. How was she going to explain this to Henry? What if he refused to have Hope at the ranch?

Hope returned with a single worn carpetbag.

"Is that all?"

"Yes, ma'am." She gripped the handle with both hands.

Bertha looked around, making sure no one else was close by. The two stood alone by the livery hitching posts.

"You should know, girl, that I used to run a bordello."

Hope's eyes grew huge. When the girl didn't run screaming, Bertha continued. "I don't do that anymore, and I'll do everything I can to make sure you never have to work that way…but some people can't forget, and you might suffer by association. If you don't want to risk that, then you can stay here in town or continue on with your wagon train."

Hope studied Bertha for a moment. "Anything is better than staying with Mr. Arnold."

Well, thought Bertha, *I guess I'm not quite the bottom of the barrel. That's a step up.*

Now, she only had to wait for Henry's reaction.

CHAPTER 22

Henry drove the wagon toward town. Without the weight of the potatoes he'd started out with, the wagon bounced uncomfortably along the rough track. It was that uncomfortable in-between time, not quite wagon weather, but not quite sled weather, either.

He'd traded the potatoes, along with some metal knives and bullets, at the Absaalooka camp south of town. The Indians were passing through on their way to their winter home.

In return for his goods, Henry got a buffalo robe for Bertha and a pair of moccasins. He hadn't planned on the shoes, but they'd reminded him of Bertha: pretty beadwork on a practical shoe. Not that he'd tell her that.

She'd done a fine job of reworking her wardrobe to be homestead-useful. But he'd noticed her boots, as fine as they made her ankles look when her skirts flashed a little high, were more pretty than practical. Sometimes she favored her feet—even working barefoot, he discovered when he came back to the cabin earlier than she expected—despite the cold. The weather would only turn colder as they headed into winter. The moccasins would be comfy and warm.

He knew some people would take offense, as poorly as they looked upon the Indians, but Bertha…she knew all kinds could act poorly, or not, and it had nothing to do with whether they were Indian or white.

As for the robe, well, winter was coming on strong. There were going to be nights when he and Charlie would need to sleep in the cabin, proprieties be damned, and so he needed to be sure Bertha could stay warm tucked in her bed in the far room.

As he approached town, he saw a long line of wagons tailing right out the eastern end. There were more people milling about than existed in the whole town.

He was surprised to see Bertha walking along the track toward him. Even more surprised to see a young gal trudging along behind her.

He halted the horses.

"Bertha?"

"Hello, Henry," she said heartily.

"Who's that?" He tipped his chin up toward the scrawny girl, who was studying the ground at her feet.

Bertha tossed her head and flipped her skirts around, a sure sign she was feeling her Big Bertha.

"I need some help at the ranch."

Henry launched out of the wagon. He'd tied the horses to a bush and asked the girl to wait there. He grabbed Bertha's hand and tucked it into his arm and hauled her away.

"What in tarnation?"

Bertha drew in closer, quietly explaining what had transpired in town.

"There's a preacher. Why can't he and his wife take her?"

"They've gone to Helena, and no one knows when they'll get back."

"So now she's going to live on my ranch?" Henry stopped in his tracks. He'd been a bachelor—alone. He'd come back from Texas to find a whole passel of women in his home. He got rid of the women, except Bertha, who he'd grown accustomed to, and she was going to leave in the spring. All these changes, and the one he wanted he couldn't have! "How long is she going to stay? What happens when you leave me?"

Henry stared at Bertha, realizing what he'd just admitted to himself. And to her. He wanted her. He wanted her in that way a man loves a woman with his body. And he wanted her in that way that his heart yearned for hers.

And she wanted Joshua.

He looked away, staring but not seeing the horizon. What the hell was he going to do? His life had turned crazy this year.

Henry returned to the present when Bertha laid her hand on his forearm. She looked up at him, beseechingly.

"Henry. I *must* help her. If she goes with that man to Virginia City, you know what's going to happen."

Henry knew it.

"What about Joshua?"

"No, she needs a woman."

"I meant—"

"I know what you meant." She had a tight set to her lips which told him Joshua wasn't happy.

"You're always going to collect strays, aren't you?"

Bertha looked startled. Henry smiled grimly to himself. He was pretty sure a life with Bertha would be full of surprises. He wondered if Joshua was up to it.

They walked back to the wagon. Bertha introduced Hope. Henry helped her up into the back of the wagon. She curled up on the buffalo robe, her feet turned so he could see the soles of her boots, which looked worn paper thin. She was so tired, she was already falling asleep.

He untied the horses and jumped up into the wagon, sitting beside Bertha. "She's going to need boots," he said.

Bertha turned to look then nodded.

He *heeyaw*ed the horses forward, turning onto Main Street. He'd pick up their purchases and see about getting some thick leather to resole the girl's boots.

Bertha sat with her knees together, turned slightly to the side. She smiled and nodded graciously to everyone they passed, and somehow Henry knew she was putting on a show and wasn't as relaxed and happy as she pretended to be.

CHAPTER 23

Bertha looked through Hope's clothes.

"Is this it?" Bertha asked. She had asked Hope to lay out her clothes on the bed. Inside the carpetbag had been one worn dress, a skirt and top, a tatty shawl, and a scratchy woolen blanket.

"Just that, ma'am. And what I'm wearing. Mr. Arnold took my best dresses for his daughters as payment for taking me along."

"What about your parents' wagon and goods?"

"He sold most of it in Wyoming. Paid the doctor and the burying man, and he said the rest was for feeding me."

"Humph," said Bertha. "Of course he did." She held the dress up to Hope. "This doesn't fit you."

"It was my mother's." Her voice caught.

Bertha examined the fabric and then the seams. "Let's see if we can alter this for you. I have a pretty ribbon that will match it." She saw the trapped look on the girl's face. She hadn't had many choices lately. "Would you like to do that? You can think about it if you need to."

Truth was, the girl would need more than one dress. But

they'd deal with that later. For now, she could borrow one of the dresses that Kit left behind. The dress would be a little big, but not much. They could alter that too.

Bertha heard the door to the cabin open and then the clatter of firewood being spilled. She said, "You think on it, Hope."

She walked into the main room to see Henry crouched by the fireplace, stacking wood. He glanced over his shoulder.

"This'll have to last you until day after tomorrow. There's a mountain lion stalking the herd, and I've got to kill it or run it off."

Bertha sighed. She could tell Henry had a bee in his bonnet. She wasn't going to head off East and leave him responsible for Hope. She'd find a place for the girl before she left in the spring. But it irritated her that Henry would think so poorly of her.

"I can split wood," Bertha said.

A ghost of a smile passed over Henry's face. He nodded and then tipped his head at Hope, who was hovering just behind Bertha. He stood, pointing to the table.

"There's a couple of pieces of leather there. You cut 'em to size, and I'll get to attaching them to Hope's boots within the week. Until we can get a proper new pair."

Bertha watched the door even after Henry left, dancing dots in front of her eyes, left over from the bright light outside. He might not want Hope here, or even Bertha for that matter, but he still did the right thing.

"Miss Bertha? I'm not used to splitting wood, but I can haul water and…and…"

Bertha smiled. "Don't worry, Hope. There's plenty of work for both of us."

They walked outside into the bright morning light, cold air breezing under their skirts.

· · ·

"Miss Bertha? Look yonder. It's that man from town."

Bertha put the axe down and held her hand over her eyes, blocking the blinding sun. Joshua rode into the yard, hat in hand and a basket tied to the saddle behind him.

"I come with a peace offering," he said as he dismounted. He untied the basket and held it out.

Bertha touched her brow and felt the damp curls. How she wished she were dressed to impress.

"Hope, take that bucket and run down to the creek, please. Take your time fetching the water."

The girl looked back and forth between Bertha and Joshua. "Yes, ma'am." She took the bucket and skipped away.

Joshua brought the basket to the bench alongside the front door. "It's a cold dinner. I wanted to make sure you had time to talk to me."

Leave it to Joshua to take away her best excuse to avoid him and remove a tiresome chore at the same time. Bertha let the corners of her mouth tip up in a small smile.

"Cut to the chase, Joshua."

He put his hands in his pockets and hunched his shoulders against the cold. "You just got rid of all the others. Why'd you take on a new girl? You were free."

Bertha realized Joshua was right. She had been free, poised to have all she'd been working for—surviving for—all these years. But she'd had no choice. Truly, even as her mind had seen all the trouble that would come with the girl, her heart had screamed at her to protect the girl.

"Hope."

"Hope for what?"

"The girl: her name is Hope. Someone had to help Hope."

"It's not your problem, Bertha. You can't save everyone. You've done your share of caring. Now it's time for you. Now it's your time to be cared for." Joshua stepped forward and put his hands on Bertha's shoulders. "You can't escape the past if you won't leave it behind you." He leaned forward and kissed her cheek.

Bertha just looked at him.

She yearned to agree with him.

But she didn't.

Joshua gently squeezed her shoulders before stepping away. "Think about it, sweetheart." He gathered the reins, mounted his horse and rode off back down the trail toward town.

Bertha took a deep breath.

She had seen the hopelessness in Hope's eyes as that man from the wagon train had tried to give her away.

Give her away. To anyone.

Hope was probably still afraid, but after walking over the mountains, and across the plains before that, she was plum worn out. She did whatever Bertha asked, and with good spirits, but she was quick to tire and in desperate need of some good food.

A cold wind blasted through the yard, whipping Bertha's hair and skirts, pushing her forward. Her own selfishness was laid bare.

What good was all that Bertha had suffered, if she couldn't use it to help this girl or others like her? Did Bertha really want to hide in an ivory tower, brushing her hair and fluffing her ruffles? How could she live with herself?

She wasn't much for church; too many people didn't approve of her. But she still had faith. She still believed. She knew she ought to look not to her own interests but the interests of others. Faith without deeds wouldn't cut it.

She had survived.

More than survived. She had thrived.

And so, if some girl like Hope landed at Bertha's feet, Bertha could not ignore her. Of course she would provide a place to sleep and food to eat so that Hope could survive and choose a better life. So that she didn't have to go through what Bertha went through.

Joshua.

She yearned to run away, to never see the darkness of life again. But she couldn't do that. And she couldn't love and respect a man who couldn't accept that part of her.

Bertha took a deep breath. Perhaps there was something she could do in St. Louis to help women there. Something more organized. She knew that there would be women in trouble.

There were always women in trouble.

She would have to convince Joshua to allow her this. Convince him that no one would discover Bertha's past just because she aided these other women. He only saw one slice of Bertha, but she was a whole pie.

Bertha felt a mix of sadness and relief. Sadness for the long-held dream that she now let go of. She could not go away and pretend she was not who she really was. That she had not done what she had really done.

She wished she had admitted this to herself sooner.

She also felt relief because she was no longer pulled in two directions. She knew what she intended to do with her future.

Bertha whirled around in the wind, feeling it cleanse and cut away the old, baring the new. Her feelings whirled still too. Sadness. Relief. And confusion.

Because she couldn't stop thinking about Henry.

CHAPTER 24

Henry watched Joshua disappear over the crest of a hill. How on earth Bertha could want to spend her life with him…he kept trying to tell himself it was the right thing for Bertha, but damn, it didn't feel that way in his gut.

He continued down his own trail. He'd found the mountain lion and shot it already. It was sickly looking, which was likely why it was tracking the cows. Now, he had fine fur wrapped up in his saddlebag, waiting to be treated when he got back home.

He heard the thwack of log splitting as he approached the cabin. He tied Nugget to the hitching post and pulled out the lion skin to show off to Bertha.

"Bertha," he called out.

He repeated her name, louder each time, trying to get her attention. She was so clearly deep in her thoughts. He didn't want to scare her while she was swinging an axe.

He waited until the axe was embedded in the log before trying again. "Beebee?"

Bertha stopped mid-swing. She looked up to see Henry.

She smiled, a full-on light-up-the-world smile.

Henry's heart fell. Whatever had happened with Joshua must have made Bertha very happy. "You look…different."

Her smile flickered.

"Happy, I mean."

Bertha tipped her head. "I think I am," she said. "What have you got there?"

Henry shook out the pelt, thick and golden.

"Oh my," said Bertha, her eyes lighting up. "Aren't you the hunter? It's beautiful."

He coughed. "Yes, I thought it might help warm the walls."

She nodded as she petted the soft fur.

"I was wondering. The skies are clearing, and the wind has stopped gusting. Would you like to ride tomorrow? The foothills down that way"—he pointed south—"overlook the town and the southeastern end of the valley. It's a fine view. With the lion taken care of and this impressive amount of wood you've split, I'd say we could take a break."

"I'd like that," Bertha said in a soft voice that had Henry leaning in ever so slightly.

THE NEXT DAY, THEY WOKE TO THE HEAVIEST HOARFROST Henry had ever seen. The sparkling white frost covered every blade of grass, every leaf and every branch so thickly it looked like it had snowed. Their brown world was suddenly spectacularly white. Everyone's chores took a little longer than usual because they kept stopping to admire the beauty.

After chores, Henry and Bertha headed out. They'd left Charlie tending the cattle and Hope hemming her mother's dress. They rode side by side. By unspoken consent, they spoke only on safe topics. They talked about the changes in the Territory they'd both seen in the past couple of years, the influx of miners and homesteaders.

After an hour, the two reached the hills. They were

different from the mountains they backed up into, softer and less jagged, like an earth blanket had been draped over them. Today, that blanket was white with the thick frost, causing the riders to squint from the reflected sun. Henry and Bertha rode up the hillside, leaning forward onto the horse's necks in the steeper spots. The view emerged slowly as they rode up.

When they reached the top, Henry watched Bertha instead of the view.

"Oh my," she said, one hand lifting to rest above her heart in awe. To their west, the valley opened up. It was a mix of sparkling white with bits of gold and brown peeking out, surrounded by white-capped mountains. She turned to Henry. "It's sublime."

The wind whipped her blond curls out from her warm hat, and the cold put roses on her cheeks. Henry couldn't breathe. The look of joy on Bertha's face made his heart stutter.

A movement in the distance caught his eye. They were not the only people to climb the hill that day. It was another couple, and they were standing with their horses in a dip behind some bushes, perhaps avoiding the wind. They led their horses out toward Henry and Bertha. Henry saw as they approached that the woman was with child. He realized he knew them.

"Cal! Amanda!" he called out. He turned to Bertha, who watched them warily. "These folks don't live too far from us."

They rode closer to the couple before dismounting.

"Henry!"

The two men shook hands. Henry gently hugged Amanda. "I don't want to injure you," he said, alluding to her delicate state.

She laughed. "I'm hardier than that, I hope."

Henry put his arm behind Bertha's back and drew her forward. "Mrs. Bertha Banks, this is Calvin Ayers and his wife, Amanda."

They greeted each other in a friendly manner, though Henry could tell Bertha was holding back.

"Henry, you're skinny as a fence post," said Cal.

"You should have seen me a month ago. Bertha's been fattening me up. I was in rough shape when I got back from Texas."

"That explains why we haven't seen you," said Amanda. She reached out and took Bertha's hand. "I received a letter from a friend in Virginia City telling me you were living at Henry's ranch. I've been looking forward to meeting you."

Bertha glanced at Henry. He could see the wheels turning in her head. She prided herself on never looking out of sorts, but he could read her now. She wasn't sure if the letter told Amanda about Bertha's business in Virginia City or not. She didn't know whether to accept the gesture of friendship or hold back.

Henry smiled encouragingly. He'd only known the couple for a year or so, when he began scouting the area for land for his homestead, but everything he'd seen said they were good folk. But he realized that every introduction would be this way for Bertha. He could see why she would want to get away.

Bertha smiled at Amanda and allowed herself to be led a few feet away. The two women looked out over the valley, Amanda pointing out landmarks.

"I heard you had quite a few people living at your ranch," said Cal carefully.

Henry nodded. "I did. We're down to four of us."

"That's too bad. I was hoping to lure one of the girls to our place to help out Amanda this spring when the baby's born."

"Actually, the girl, Hope. She's about thirteen. She'd be a good helper."

Amanda called over. "Oh, we couldn't take Bertha's helper away."

"Bertha's leaving this spring anyway. She won't mind,"

Henry blurted out. Everyone stared at him. "I'll be glad to get space back from all these womenfolk," he mumbled, realizing he looked like a jerk, and it wasn't even the truth.

Amanda and Bertha both glared at him. Cal let out a low whistle.

"Come on, Bertha. Let's look at the view in that direction." The two women walked off together, their skirts leaving a trail where they knocked the frost off the grasses.

Henry had wanted to show Bertha the view. To show her the town from up high, point out the newest buildings and also show her where the Indian encampment had been.

He had looked forward to watching Bertha's face light up.

He kicked a knobby root poking out of the ground.

"What are you doing, Henry?" asked Cal.

"Hell if I know," said Henry. "Hell if I know."

The horse slipped on the icy rock, lurching to the side. One rein was pulled from Bertha's hands, stiff from the cold. She reached down the horse's neck to grab the swinging rein before the horse decided to run with its freedom. She shivered as the frigid wind slid past her collar and down her back.

She couldn't wait to get back to the cabin and a warm fire. She'd wrap herself in the buffalo robe that Henry had given her and roast her toes in the fireplace. Hope was manning the fire and would have a hot pot of coffee waiting. Bertha smiled. Perhaps she'd break out the whiskey when Henry and Charlie got back.

She'd helped them round up the bulk of the herd and push them into a canyon that would protect them from the worst of the storm that was pushing down on them. But the two men had remained to bring in a few strays. There was something about the sky, dark as dusk at midday, which forewarned of a nasty storm ahead. Whether it would be icy rain or snow, all the animals needed to hunker down.

For now, it looked to be turning to ice. At the fork, Bertha decided to take the slightly longer but less steep route down the hill. She and the horse travelled a quarter mile out of the way. At the creek crossing, the horse shied, nearly unseating Bertha.

Her first instinct was to fear another mountain lion, but as her horse danced about, she could see from her high perch past a downed log the muted colors of a woolen blanket, covered with sprinkles of ice and shivering in a ball.

"Halloo," Bertha called out. The blanketed ball stilled for a moment, but then the shivers started again.

"Halloo," she repeated. "I see you there. This is no day to be out."

The blanket slid back to reveal wet hair plastered around the face of an Indian girl, perhaps ten years old. Her eyes were wide with fear and pain. The girl's teeth chattered, and her fists clutched the blanket.

"Do you speak English?"

The girl only looked at Bertha.

"Where are your people?" Bertha looked around, but that was futile, for little could be seen in the icy rain except the occasional snowflake. She wasn't sure where the girl's tribe was, but since Henry would have known if there was an encampment nearby, she doubted the girl would make it there in the storm. She knew bringing home an Indian girl might not be the smartest thing to do, but what other choice was there?

"Come on." Bertha waved the girl toward her and patted the back of her horse. "Come with me."

The Indian girl's eyes opened wider. Bertha waved her over again. At the girl's hesitation, Bertha pointed at the clouds, mimed rain with her fingers and then wrapped her arms around her middle and pretended to shiver. It wasn't hard to pretend. Finally, she held out her hand to the girl.

After a long moment, the girl uncurled herself. Her dress was soaked through, the suede freezing and turning stiff in the bitter air. She limped toward the horse. Bertha couldn't tell if she was injured or just frozen stiff. Bertha shook her outstretched hand. The girl stood just out of reach and studied Bertha, clutching the blanket around her.

Bertha wanted to reassure her, to smile and tell her it would be all right, but nothing felt right about smiling right now. She could only hope the girl could tell Bertha meant her no harm.

Finally, the girl stepped forward to put her cold, bare hand into Bertha's gloved one. Bertha pulled her up behind the saddle.

"Hold on," she said, though she doubted the girl understood her. She squeezed the mare's sides with her legs and clucked her forward. The girl grabbed the sides of Bertha's coat and hung on.

The mare trudged across the creek and down out of the foothills. The two riders hunched against the sharp ice crystals whipping at any exposed skin. The mare picked up speed as they got closer to the ranch.

Bertha felt relief as she recognized the dark outline of the cabin. Thank goodness the horse knew the way. A rectangle of yellow-orange pierced the gray as the cabin door opened and the bulky shape of Henry burst out.

He rushed over to Bertha, reaching out to grab hold of her hands, squeezing gently.

"I have been worried sick—"

He stopped when he saw Bertha's travelling companion. His eyes widened. He looked back at Bertha but didn't say anything.

Bertha could feel the weight of the girl, leaning away from Henry.

He shook his head, just slightly. He pulled the reins from her frozen fingers.

In a quieter voice he said, "You two get inside. I'll take care of the horse."

He helped Bertha dismount. He turned to the girl, who cringed when he held out his hands to her.

"It's alright, girly," said Bertha. "Let him help you."

The girl looked around, scared.

Henry said something in a language that Bertha didn't recognize. Just a few words, but it was enough. Or perhaps it was the promise of the warm fire just steps away, but the girl leaned forward and slid into Henry's hands. He put her down gently, immediately removing his hands.

"Come along," Bertha added, leading the way into the cabin.

She glanced back at Henry, but in the icy rain she couldn't see him well enough to tell how he felt about her newest rescue.

Inside, Hope and Charlie were waiting, huddled around the fire. Hope gave a little shriek, jumping behind Charlie when she saw the Indian girl. Charlie stood tall, protecting Hope.

From a child.

A wave of exhaustion rolled over Bertha.

"Don't be foolish, you two." She reached behind the girl to pull the door closed. She pointed to the fireplace. "Go warm yourself there." The girl sidestepped toward the fire, never turning her back to the others.

Hope peeked over Charlie's shoulder. "Henry was mighty concerned when he arrived back here before you." Charlie nodded vigorously.

Bertha continued to untoggle her sodden coat. She ought not to be pleased that she'd worried Henry, but truth was it gave her a little warm glow to know Henry cared about her. She was glad he'd made it back safely too.

She finally pushed the coat off her shoulders and let it fall to the floor. "Hope, sugar, will you take care of that? I'm going to put on dry clothes." As hard as it was to leave the warmth of the front room, it was harder to get her fingers to work on the smaller buttons and ties of her clothes. By the time she was finished, she could hear Henry return.

Bertha emerged from the bedroom. She brought her thick buffalo-skin robe that Henry had given her. Oh, she wanted to wrap herself in it, but instead, she carried it across the room and wrapped it around the Indian girl. Bertha knew there was no way that girl was going to strip out of her own clothes in the cabin of white people, despite the cold and wet. All Bertha could do was help her warm up and dry out as best she could.

"Hand out that coffee, why don't you?" Bertha said to Hope. At Hope's inquiring look, she added, "Well, offer it to the girl, Hope, and see if she wants some."

Hope held out a tin cup filled with hot coffee. The Indian girl looked at the cup, then at Hope, and then at Bertha. Bertha nodded slightly. The girl took the cup, the two carefully trading the cup without touching each other.

Bertha turned to Henry, who was shaking off his hair now that the ice crystals were melting. She smiled. "I'm sorry I worried you." She explained her detour and how she found the Indian girl.

Henry nodded but was still tense. "Dammit, Bertha, you can't go wandering off in a storm like that. It's afternoon, sure, but it might as well be the middle of the night."

He reached out his hands.

For one brief moment, Bertha thought he was going to pull her into his arms. She leaned forward ever so slightly.

But he didn't. He turned to Hope and snatched up a cup of coffee. She leaned back, ever so slightly.

"There could be trouble," he said, staring into the dark liquid.

Bertha thought of all the stories she'd heard of Indians attacking whites and how worried someone must be over the girl. Of course there could be trouble. She knew that. But what else could she have done?

"I couldn't leave the child to freeze to death, Henry. I don't think you would have, either."

Henry continued to study his coffee. "Joshua isn't going to like this."

Bertha's heart sank. That was the trouble he was worried about. She was worried about Indian attacks, and he was worried about whether she was jeopardizing her relationship with Joshua. Worried about whether she'd be gone from his ranch as quickly as possible.

Not life or death, but how soon he could get rid of Bertha.

She took a deep breath. Sometimes she thought Henry cared about her. Sometimes she thought he was looking forward to her emigrating back East.

Her heart cracked.

She wanted Henry to care.

To love her.

She wanted it unreasonably so.

CHAPTER 26

Henry shielded his eyes from the bright light. The storm had passed in the early morning hours, leaving a blanket of snow that covered everything. All the clouds had blown away, leaving a bright-blue sky and a light that reflected off the white from every direction.

The glare didn't seem to bother his horse as much as it bothered Henry, but luckily the horse knew the way to the small, protective canyon where they'd left the cattle yesterday. The surefooted animal wasn't bothered by the snow in any way.

He'd had Charlie stay back at the cabin, shoveling the yard and the most necessary paths. Charlie had puffed out his chest and assured Henry that he'd protect the women, even while his eyes had fearfully darted about in search of Indian war parties.

Hope, being not much older than the Indian girl, had taken to her presence better. The last he'd seen, the two girls had been cozied up to the fireplace, enjoying its warmth, while pointing to objects around the room and saying the names in their respective languages.

And Bertha.

Ah, Bertha.

Henry sighed. He'd been worried to pieces when he returned yesterday and realized she hadn't made it home. He'd wanted to throttle her and hug her at the same time.

And he was confused. She said that she wanted a certain future with Joshua…but she kept doing things contrary to everything Joshua wanted and could possibly ruin things for her. He didn't see how she and Joshua were compatible.

Truth was, Henry couldn't see Bertha taking any other action. She had such a big heart; there was no way she'd leave a child to freeze in the storm. That damn fool Joshua ought to accept it. Hell, he ought to embrace it.

A movement in the distance caught Henry's eye and interrupted his thoughts. Three riders. He squinted. Indians. Crow. Likely they were looking for the girl. Henry swung Nugget in their direction.

The three Crow headed toward Henry. Upon meeting, he was able, in his limited Crow language, to say what he hoped was the equivalent of "Find girl. Come home."

He led them back to his homestead.

As they entered the yard, Bertha stepped out of the cabin. He could tell by the way she held her shawl that she also gripped her small pistol. He gave a slight shake of his head and watched as her shoulders sagged in relief and her pocket sagged with the weight of the gun dropping into it.

"They're looking for the girl."

Bertha stepped aside, and the door behind her opened. The Indian girl hobbled outside. She was dry finally, thankfully. Her hair was neat and freshly braided. He wasn't sure if Bertha or Hope was to thank for that.

The girl smiled and hurried forward, only to stop short as a flash of pain crossed her face as her foot reminded her of its injury. Bertha took her arm and carefully led her to the man who had stepped his horse forward at the first sight of the girl.

At the side of his horse, the girl turned to Bertha and said thank you in her own language. Henry didn't think Bertha knew any of the Crow language, but that didn't seem to matter.

"You're very welcome, sweet pea," Bertha said with a gentle smile. She glanced up at the man on the horse but didn't say anything else. She turned and walked back to stand in front of the cabin door. Henry saw Hope peeking over her shoulder.

The men thanked Henry and his family for caring for the girl. Henry didn't say it wasn't his family. He doubted he could explain the various relationships in the cabin even if he knew the words in their language.

They all watched the three men and the young girl leave. She glanced over her shoulder once, a small smile directed at Bertha.

Once out of sight, Henry walked the horse up to Bertha. He tipped his hat. "You done good."

A brilliant smile lit up Bertha's face. Damn, that woman had a big smile. A big heart. A big…figure. Everything about her was big and bold and wonderful. He was tempted to lean down and kiss her.

Bertha looked up at him through her long lashes. "Henry, there's something—"

"Hey, boss," interrupted Charlie, walking up the path from the creek with a bucket in each hand. "You didn't need to come back and check on us. I've got my eyes peeled."

Bertha laughed outright, while Henry just shook his head.

"You were going to say?" he asked.

"Never mind," she said. She waved her hands. "Shoo, you go on now. Back to your cows."

Henry turned the horse and headed back out to his cattle.

He found himself still shaking his head as he rode. Some of it was for Charlie. As good as the young man was with the cattle, he didn't have any frontier-living sense.

But some of that head shaking was for himself. He cared about Bertha. So much that he wanted what was best for her. Even if he didn't think her choice was the right one. All he knew for sure was that he was an idiot for making it easier for her to leave him.

CHAPTER 27

Two days later, Bertha rode into town. She'd chosen one of her town dresses. Back in Virginia City, she'd worn her skirts a mite short to show off her ankles, as well as to avoid the mud and dirt. On the ranch, she'd elected to keep them short so as not to drag them through the dirt and mud as she worked. But she'd added ruffles and lace to her town dresses to make them a mite longer, and now, as the last storm's snow melted and created a mud slurry, she was thinking how impractical it was. She had to lift her skirts up anyway, just to keep them clean.

She'd dressed with care out of respect for Joshua and the many kindnesses he'd offered her. She wore her second favorite dress, a green velvet one that warmed her on this cold day, though with some extra fabric to make it more modest.

They needed to have a discussion. She realized that with Hope and the Indian girl…she needed to be able to do what she needed to do. Joshua tried to let her be, but he wanted her to be someone she couldn't be. There was a part of her that wanted to go with Joshua and become the woman she was supposed to have become: a respectable wife. But her life had taken a drastic turn when she was sixteen.

Henry was right. She couldn't pretend that the last fourteen years hadn't happened. She was who she was.

She strode toward the hotel, ready to get the conversation over with. Just as she reached the farrier's building, a couple stepped out of the mercantile. The man turned his wife back in toward the store. As they reentered the store, Bertha heard him mutter, "Only one type of woman wears clothes like that out here."

There was a hitch in her step, but otherwise she kept moving forward. She thought of the dress she had made over for Hope. It was a fabric a bit grand for an orphan girl on the frontier, but would that mark her in the eyes of some? Did it matter? Bertha would prefer honest scorn to a respectability built on lies and hemmed in by the moral opinions of others.

She realized she couldn't please everyone. But she could please herself…and interestingly, that seemed to be fine with Henry.

She entered the lobby of the hotel. Immediately, Joshua appeared and strongly led her to the back room. He immediately set to pouring them each a glass of whiskey.

"Joshua," Bertha began, "there's something I need to tell you."

"Charlie came to town yesterday. I already heard about your most recent stray. What were you thinking, Bertha? You're putting lives in danger." He handed her a glass.

She scoffed. "That's ridiculous."

Joshua's face reddened. "It's not ridiculous, and I'm not going to put up with it."

Bertha took a sip of her whiskey, trying to decide how to proceed. At least now her feelings of guilt were dissipating. "That's what I'm here to discuss with you. You won't have to put up with it." She took a deep breath. "I'm not going to St. Louis with you. I'm going to stay here."

Joshua's face turned thunderous. "With Henry?"

"We haven't discussed that." God, she thought to herself, I may be making the mistake of my life. But I'll survive. I always do. "You're offering me a secure life. A pampered life. But I need more than that."

Joshua waved away her concerns. "Look, we'll find you some little charities to support in St. Louis. You can help others, just at more of a distance. I'll pamper you, and we'll enjoy the good life."

Bertha thought of him pushing her to shed her charges. It wasn't for her. It was for him. He wanted her attention, her focus.

"It's time for the new you." He put his glass down. "Come on, sweetheart," Joshua crooned as he reached out his arms to embrace her.

Bertha stayed put, clasping her hands together. She tipped her head, studying Joshua. He wanted, it seemed, the new Bertha more than even Bertha did. "It turns out, Joshua, that I can't simply bury Big Bertha in the past. And she's not all bad. 'Don't throw the baby out with the bath water,' you know the saying."

Joshua grew still as she spoke. He clenched his jaw. "A better saying is, 'Don't dig for water under the outhouse'."

Bertha drew back as if she had been slapped.

Suddenly, she realized what she ought to have seen long ago. No matter whether Bertha wanted to forget her past, Joshua never would. It would be lurking just under the surface, his disdain and his fear of the truth being revealed. No matter how hard she tried to whitewash her past, she would never be good enough for Joshua. He knew her history.

And he would never forget.

Bertha reached deep down inside, pulling her Big Bertha

mantle across her heart. She pushed his hands away. "I told you I came here to break it off. I told you I need more. I meant it, even before I realized what a dastardly ass you are."

The whites of his eyes flashed as he realized how angry Bertha was. He grabbed her hand and squeezed.

"I already bought a house for you. What have you got to do here? Don't think that Henry is going to marry you," Joshua hissed at her.

Bertha tossed her drink in his face.

Joshua yanked her hand hard, half dragging her across the chair. His other hand grabbed the nape of her neck. Anger and pride warred in Joshua's red face. The whiskey dripped down, leaving little streams of yellow across his shirt front.

"You're not listening to me, Big Bertha. Unless you're going back into business, you'd better come with me."

Bertha looked him straight in the eye. She slid her little pearl-handled knife from her skirt pocket with her free hand. Joshua's nasty expression froze when she pressed it into his stomach.

"You're not listening to *me*. I came to say goodbye." She pushed the knife harder into his stomach until he released her neck and hand. She stepped back, never taking her eyes from his. "I could never marry you now."

Joshua froze. A sly smile crossed his face. "Marry you? I was never going to marry you. I said I'd give you a house and a new name. But not my name."

Every conversation they'd ever had ran through Bertha's mind. He'd never actually proposed, but he had alluded to their future in such a way that it was implied. She wondered if he had been leading her along the entire time, or if he was trying to save face now.

It didn't matter.

She stepped quickly from the room. She was glad she had planned on a short visit and not unsaddled the horse. She walked directly to the hitching post, untethered her horse and mounted. It was all she could do to appear calm and collected. She wanted to run and scream. Scream at Joshua. Scream at the world. Scream at herself.

She gathered the reins and turned the horse. She nodded to a passerby. She walked the horse down Main Street, anxious to get out of view. She wanted only to run back to the ranch. To safety. To Henry. Who she couldn't even discuss this with. He'd think she turned to him because Joshua had rejected her.

Bertha smiled bitterly to herself. She thought she knew men so well, but she had misjudged Joshua for so long. Her heart wasn't broken. She'd already given that to Henry. But it was bruised. She was hurt that her friend wasn't her friend. She'd trusted Joshua. He didn't love her; she'd never thought he did. But he was pragmatic and said the things she'd wanted to hear. And she'd willfully ignored the things he hadn't said, but should have.

Bertha wanted to kick herself. She was relieved she'd broken it off with Joshua. Grateful that she'd learned the true situation before she'd arrived in St. Louis. Happy, even, because all the questions that had been swirling inside of her were settled.

She belonged here. Everyone knew her history. Accept it or not, there would be no surprises. The West was full of people reinventing themselves, and she would do so again, but honestly and openly. She would not pretend to be someone she was not.

Bertha pulled the horse to a stop. She looked back at the town in the distance. No one was following. She didn't think Joshua would, but then she'd been wrong about him before. She looked ahead, toward home. Henry's ranch. She couldn't see it from where she was, but it called to her.

Who was she? What kind of life could she carve out for herself? Could it be with Henry?

Bertha took a deep breath. She was finally willing to accept who she was. She could not move to some new place and pretend her life hadn't happened. That she had jumped through time, from the wagon train heading to California with her intended's family, to St. Louis as a wife and charity volunteer. That wouldn't work. It couldn't. She didn't have to go back to a brothel, but she had to accept that Big Bertha was a part of her. Not who she was now, but a slice of her.

Bertha nudged the horse forward. Henry. She'd been so excited when she left the ranch. Sad, of course, because she thought that Joshua would be hurt by her rejection. But it seemed only his pride was hurt. But excited because she'd planned to return to the ranch, to Henry, a free woman. To declare herself, as it were. She wasn't sure Henry felt the same, especially since she'd rejected him once. But she was a woman who had survived by making things happen, and she was fully prepared to do that again.

But now…now how could Henry ever believe she wanted him? He would think that she was choosing him because it didn't work out with Joshua.

And if she were being honest with herself, Bertha felt doubt. She'd been so wrong about Joshua. Was she wrong about Henry too?

CHAPTER 28

"Alright, Beebee, I've made some work for you." Henry put a smile in his voice, hoping his news would cheer her up. She'd been distant and distracted since she returned from town yesterday.

Bertha loosened the saddle girth and looked up with a smile that didn't reach her eyes. It didn't seem her morning ride had cheered her up any.

Henry walked toward her.

"It must be bad if you're trying to sweet-talk me with my childhood nickname."

He leaned against the top rail of the fence. "Not bad at all, I hope you'll agree. But a bit of work."

Bertha crossed her arms and frowned like she was upset by the news. Even so, a smile tugged at the corners of her mouth. A real one, this time. She raised her eyebrows and waited.

"You remember Cal and Amanda?"

Bertha nodded.

"I came across Cal earlier today. He was out hunting elk. We got to talking, and he mentioned how lonely Amanda is for female company."

Bertha waved her hand to speed up the story.

"So, given the date, I invited them to have Thanksgiving dinner with us," he explained. "I've been thinking about Thanksgiving since we discussed it with Dorothea. It's too far for that family to travel at this time of year, but Cal and Amanda are only a few miles away."

Bertha remained silent, waiting to hear if there was more to this plan.

"Just the two of them?" she asked.

"And Hope and Charlie too."

"So, I've got to serve a fancy dinner for six? The day after tomorrow?"

Henry eyed her, unable to tell how she felt about this. Finally, he responded. "Yes, that's about right."

Bertha looked at Henry with assessing eyes. He found himself wanting to shuffle about like a schoolboy caught out by the teacher. He wasn't sure what was going through her head, but it seemed to be about more than a Thanksgiving dinner. Even the horse shifted on her feet.

"Beebee?" He looked into her beautiful eyes. This morning, they were less gray with the blue standing out more. He loved how they changed with her moods.

Bertha released her crossed arms and put her hands on her hips as she lightly shook her head. "You're nothing but trouble, Henry."

He felt a wave of relief. "Maybe not 'nothing but'."

Bertha stared at him a moment, opened her mouth to speak, and instead she grabbed the saddle off the horse's back. Henry reached out to take it from her and saw her shoulder hitch. She grimaced.

He dropped the saddle onto the railing. "What's ailing you?" He touched her arm, just below her shoulder. She winced.

She twisted away. "It's nothing. I slept on it funny is all."

Something didn't feel quite right, but Henry wasn't sure why. But he could tell Bertha wasn't going to discuss it.

"All righty," he said. "How about Thursday? What do you need?"

"I'd like some fresh venison and perhaps a couple of birds. You best get to hunting."

"But around here, Beebee? I don't want you lifting anything heavy while your arm is out of sorts."

"I'll be fine, Henry. Hope is here, and Charlie's about often enough." She waved her hands at him. "Now, shoo. Go on then. I'm going to turn this horse loose and then go select our very best potatoes. Oh, and I'd better bake more bread."

"No need for that," Henry blurted out.

Bertha reached out and smacked his arm.

Henry grinned and skedaddled out of reach before she could smack him again. He left Bertha to finish untacking her horse. He was, he realized, walking toward the cabin with a little pep in his step. She'd said 'our' potatoes.

With a nice buck deer and a couple of grouse, Henry was feeling mighty pleased with his hunting trip. It was only midafternoon, and he was heading home. He'd already gutted the deer, but if he got it hung today, he'd be able to start carving it up first thing in the morning.

As he crossed the creek, he saw another rider coming in on the path from town. He couldn't see the rider clearly but recognized Joshua's horse. He felt jealousy grab hold. He didn't want Joshua coming to sweet-talk Bertha, especially when she seemed so...vulnerable. He'd been thinking all morning about Bertha and only just realized now that was what seemed off about her. She put forth a face of capability and strength; it was easy to forget she might have moments too.

Both men pulled up when their horses met at the Y. Henry nodded. "Joshua."

"Henry."

Joshua looked him up and down, his eyes lingering on the blood, fur, and feathers. Henry waited. He wasn't going to glad-hand Joshua and act like he was happy to see him.

"I don't know what she told you. You know how women are—especially one with her background. But she had no cause for pulling that knife on me."

Henry's mind flashed back to Bertha, wincing when he touched her arm.

Now, looking at Joshua, Henry felt a tide of red sweep over him. He didn't know exactly what had happened between them, but he had a pretty good idea. His hands fisted involuntarily, causing his horse to dance in place. He brought the horse under control and turned his attention back to what Joshua was saying.

"I'm sure she told you it's over between us, but I'm going to give her another chance." There was a weird earnestness in Joshua, a combination of bruised pride and utter belief in his own prediction. "Why she thought we'd be marrying, I don't know, but I do know she'll never have another chance for a good life if she turns me down again."

Henry wanted to knock Joshua's block off.

He'd been leading Bertha on.

He wanted to beat that dastard to a pulp. But Bertha wouldn't like that.

One thing he knew about Bertha: she didn't want any man making decisions for her.

A flicker of hope ran through Henry. He wasn't sure what Bertha wanted, but he was pretty sure she didn't want to be a kept woman. And Henry sure as hell knew that he wanted Bertha. He needed a plan, and time to work on Bertha, before Joshua renewed his attentions. Not that he thought Bertha would go with the bum, but he wanted Bertha to choose Henry.

He knew better than to make decisions for Bertha…but he could stack the deck in his own favor.

"Now might not be the right time for that conversation," said Henry.

"You don't have to help me, Henry," snapped Joshua, "but this is your chance to make sure she leaves your place as planned. Otherwise, you may find yourself with a guest you can't get rid of…and all her strays."

"I hear you. I'm just saying she's preparing for guests, and I'm sure you'd rather have her full attention. Plus, she's still madder than a hornet."

"Oh sure, oh sure," said Joshua cautiously. "I can let her stew a bit longer."

Dang it, thought Henry. Joshua wouldn't wait if he thought Henry was trying to keep him away.

"Friday," said Henry. "You can't let her think you're running back to her with your tail between your legs. But any longer, and she'll get her back up even more."

Joshua tipped his hat, satisfied. "Point taken. I'll be there Friday morning." He spun his horse around, jabbed his bootheels into its sides, and took off at a canter.

Henry's eyes narrowed as he watched Joshua ride off. He still wanted to knock that fellow right off his horse.

Bertha. Henry wanted her.

He wanted her in his life. In his home. In his bed.

He just knew that life with Bertha would be so much better than life without her. He saw her brilliant smile. He heard her joyous laugh. He smiled at her wit and sass.

The good news was that Joshua was doing a fine job culling himself from the running. But that alone wouldn't convince Bertha to stay with Henry. Life on the ranch would be hard— much harder than the life of ease she'd expected to have with

Joshua. She could still head East, on her own, and make a life for herself. A life where people didn't know her past. Where no one would say, as Joshua just had, "one with her background," or cross the street or refuse to acknowledge her.

Henry wasn't sure of his next step except that he knew that he didn't want to spend the winter in a tug of war with Joshua. He wanted to spend it with Bertha in his arms.

But how was Henry going to convince her to stay with him? To marry him. She'd never do it if she felt like she had no choice. She'd fight the most then.

Well, he'd figure it out. He rode off for home, excited to see Bertha again.

CHAPTER 29

Bertha surveyed the board loaded with food. Henry and Charlie had laid it across two sawhorses, giving her the space she needed. The potatoes were mashed and awaiting a warm-up. The apple and raisin tart smelled heavenly. It would have been a mite easier if she'd had a proper oven to cook in. A loaf of bread that rose high on one end and lay flat on the other. She'd place it right in front of Henry. Huckleberry preserves. Mixed pickles. The onions were peeled, ready to be boiled. The grouse were cooked and cooling, the skin crackled and crisp.

She turned to the firepit. Hope sat on a stool, slowly turning the venison haunch on the spit. The sun shone brightly, having melted off the morning frost hours before. The breeze might have made it cold, but Bertha and Hope were plenty warm from the fire they worked over.

Bertha smiled. She'd never had a Thanksgiving Day party before. Last year, she and her girls had simply added an extra thanks to their grace when they ate their regular supper.

This made her think of Kit. Oh, how Bertha missed her. Did she do right by Kit? She'd sent Kit away to be the woman she could have been if her mother hadn't died in a mining camp, leaving Kit to be raised by a fancy lady. She'd been so sure that was the right path. But now Bertha wondered. She couldn't hide her own past, and she wasn't sure she wanted to anymore.

Had she set Kit up to suffer, having to hide her own history? Kit was young enough to adapt. But maybe she didn't want to. Bertha would write to her. Tell her that she was welcome to come back and live with Bertha.

And where would that be? Not with Joshua in St. Louis. Bertha couldn't change the way people thought about her, but she didn't have to tie herself to them, either. She could file for her own homestead. If she never married, it would be hers till she died.

And what about Henry? He was looking so handsome, freshly shaved and in his best clothes. He'd been so sweet to her the past two days…almost like he was courting her. She knew he found her attractive, but she also knew he planned to marry and have a family. Perhaps if she just stayed here and never left, he'd go along with it. She smiled ruefully to herself. That wasn't her style, nor his.

"They're here!"

Bertha heard Hope call out at the same time that she heard the bark of a dog on the crisp midday breeze. A brown-and-white dog raced into the yard, followed by Cal on his horse and Amanda on hers. They had baskets and blankets tied all around them.

Smiles wreathed everyone's faces. Bertha knew how they felt. When you lived out of town, any visiting was quite a treat.

After greetings, they unloaded the horses.

"We've brought bread and some preserves," said Amanda as Cal untied a big basket.

"And this is a honey cake," she added as Cal carefully extracted a board with a cloth tied around it.

He held it out to Bertha.

Bertha untied the twine and lifted the cloth to see a golden cake shaped like…a rabbit! She smiled. She had heard of these cakes shaped like animals, but had never seen one.

Hope ran the basket and cake board inside the cabin, rushing back out so she wouldn't miss any of the excitement.

"And don't forget this!" Cal hefted a big jug. The men slapped each other's backs as they laughed. "I made it myself."

"To help fatten you up, Henry," said Amanda, and they all laughed again.

Bertha watched the "perfect" family—a lovely couple with a baby on the way— recognizing that this was what she'd always wished for. She wanted it, but she couldn't have it.

What she could do, though, was stop herself from getting hurt.

The men left to tour the property, Charlie trailing them. Not as old as the two men, but no longer a boy. Henry proudly pointed out his improvements as they walked.

Bertha asked Hope to take the dog down to the creek.

"I'll see that he gets water," Hope called out as she raced away, the dog at her heels.

"Amanda." Bertha took a deep breath. "I am so grateful that you are here today, but there is something I must tell you. You may wish you knew before you arrived, and if you want to leave, I will understand."

Amanda drew her chin in and tilted her head. "Yes?"

"I think you ought to know…before I came here…" This was harder than she expected. "Back in Virginia City…I was… I was…"

"You were Big Bertha, no?" Amanda asked gently.

"You know?"

"You have a reputation." She spoke slowly, choosing her words with care.

Bertha's heart sank. She looked down at her hands, tightly clasped.

"Well, there's this." Amanda waved her hands in circles in front of Bertha's bosom. "Your figure."

"Oh."

"That's the past, right?"

Bertha nodded.

"You also have a reputation for helping people."

Bertha looked up. That wasn't what she expected.

"I had a letter last week from Josie. You know her, I think. She and Reg own a mercantile, and they hear all the gossip. It seems Gimpy Pete's family finally arrived. He is taking them to Helena, to Last Chance Gulch. He's told several people how you helped him." Amanda tilted her head the other way. "And a Welshman named Cadoc has been helping Delia at her washateria in return for J.B. helping him with his claim. You, apparently, suggested Cadoc seek out J.B."

Bertha was mesmerized. She never imagined that people could look at her with anything but condemnation.

Amanda smiled and took Bertha's hands into her own. "You have a reputation for caring."

The acceptance of this woman touched Bertha to the core. She brushed a tear from her eye.

"Thank you," Bertha whispered. Then, louder, she added, "Now, let's prepare the dinner."

HENRY STOOD AT THE HEAD OF THE TABLE. CAL SAT BESIDE HIM with Charlie between Cal and Bertha, who sat at the foot of the table. On her other side sat Amanda and then Hope.

"Before we eat—"

Charlie and Hope groaned.

"Hush," shushed Bertha.

"Before we eat, I have something to say. I'm mighty

thankful that we're all here together. It's been a good year, and it's right to be grateful." Henry paused to look right at Bertha. "But I won't be thankful next year, Beebee, if you're not here with me."

She stared at him, still as a rabbit. She was vaguely aware of the smiles growing around the table.

"I love you, Beebee, and I want you to stay. To be my wife and grow our homestead together."

Her heart fluttered. "But—"

"But it'll be a much harder life than if you go live in St. Louis. I know, Beebee…but we'll be together."

"But—" Bertha held up her hand when Henry opened his mouth to keep speaking. She glanced around the table but didn't let their audience stop her. "But you said you wanted a family."

"I know what I said, but family comes in many forms." He gestured at Hope and Charlie. "I have a feeling you'll be bringing many more into our family."

Henry began to walk around the table, toward Bertha. Amanda was grinning beside her, and Hope was giggling, and this was everything Bertha wanted, but she didn't know if she could believe it. Was she dreaming?

Bertha stood up. Henry took her hands. She felt the warm calluses and knew this wasn't a dream. She stared at them a moment and then looked into his eyes, trying to read his sincerity. Or sanity.

"I'll build you a whole orphanage for your strays, if that's what it takes, Beebee. I love you."

"Are you sure?" she asked, wanting so much to believe in him.

"We can't separate from our pasts. They helped make us who we are, both the good and the bad. But that stuff that you did in your past—that I did in my past—that's not who we are."

"It's just stuff we did," Bertha whispered.

"You have such a big heart, Beebee," Henry whispered back. "Share it with me."

"I've already given my big heart to you." Tears hovered on Bertha's eyelashes.

Henry grabbed Bertha and spun her around, kissing her with all his heart. Behind them, he heard cheers from their friends and family.

CHAPTER 30

Bertha slid a slice of apple pie onto the plate. Immediately, Hope grabbed the plate and dug her fork into the pie.

"What if I don't like it there?" mumbled Hope through a mouthful of food.

"You met Amanda and Cal yesterday. Do you truly think you won't like living with them?"

"Well, no. But what if I don't?"

"We've agreed only that you'll go to help out a few weeks before the baby is due and for a couple of months after the baby is born." Bertha slid another slice of pie onto her own plate and set to eating.

She had not stopped smiling since yesterday's dinner. To know Henry loved her and wanted to be with her for the rest of their lives…it was unbelievable. And yet it felt so right. For so many years, she had questioned and strived…and suddenly, there was no question. No better "something" to strive for. Everything felt right.

She looked across the table at Hope and saw the uncertainty in the girl's eyes. Twelve was such a hard age. Part child, part woman, Hope knew enough to know she had little control over her own life.

Bertha put down her fork and reached out to cover Hope's hand with her own.

"I will come check on you. And I will bring you back here if need be."

Hope turned her hand and gripped Bertha's tightly. "But—"

"I will bring you home. *We* will bring you home," Bertha said.

Hope relaxed, releasing Bertha's hand and returning to her breakfast.

Bertha smiled to herself. She wasn't sure which felt better to say: "we" or "home." Henry and Charlie had ridden out after their own pie breakfasts to check on the cattle. Before he left, Henry had kissed Bertha and said, "I'll be home soon." It wasn't just the ranch or the homestead anymore, for either of them. It was home.

"Maybe with a puppy. I heard Cal telling Henry he'd be on the lookout for a puppy for you and—" Hope broke off, hearing a sound from out in the yard at the same time Bertha did.

Bertha began to rise, but before she was even standing, she heard her name called out.

"Bertha!"

It was Joshua. He sounded angry.

Hope looked scared.

"Wait here, sweet pea," said Bertha. She put on her coat and slid a knife into the pocket, hoping she wouldn't need it. She walked outside, firmly closing the door behind her.

Joshua was dismounting. When he turned to face Bertha, she gasped. He had a bloody nose, a fat lip, and what looked like the beginnings of a black eye.

Joshua didn't bother to tie his horse up. He stomped

toward Bertha, pulling the horse along behind him. "Is it true?" he spat out. "Are you going to stay here with Henry?" He flung one arm out, encompassing the cabin and the yard in one motion. He took another menacing step toward Bertha.

Bertha realized Joshua must have run into Henry this morning. She wondered what Joshua had said to make Henry want to take it out so thoroughly on his face.

She took a step forward. She knew from experience that you couldn't let a bully think you were scared.

"You're going to regret it, you—" Joshua reached out to grab her.

Bertha hauled her arm back and let fly her fist right into Joshua's eye. She'd gotten stronger, working like a pioneer, and Joshua spun around at the impact.

"Now he's going to have a matching set."

Bertha looked past Joshua to see Henry riding into the yard. He smiled at Bertha, but it was tight, and she could tell he was still awfully angry. He leaned forward in his saddle, resting his arm on the saddle pommel.

"I guess you didn't get my message earlier, Reynolds. Let me be clear." Whatever hint of a smile had been left on his face disappeared. "I don't want to ever see you on my property or near Bertha ever again. If I do, I will beat the tar out of you."

Joshua glanced from Henry to Bertha. After a moment, he skittered to his horse, mounted and turned away. They watched him ride off toward town, wincing as he touched the skin around his eye.

Bertha smiled at Henry. "Tough guy."

"When it comes to you." He smiled back. "Not that you need me."

Bertha felt the corners of her mouth tip up. "Oh, I need you, Henry."

Henry grinned.

Then, she turned serious. "Forever and always."

Henry rode across the yard, reached down and swept Bertha up into his arms, kissing her with all his love.

Dear Kit,

Yes, I am writing to Kit. Not Catherine. I was wrong to push you to be someone you are not. I am so sorry. I wanted, and still want, only the best for you. I was so certain that going East where you could rein-vent yourself was the only way you could have a good life. But I realize now that who you were in the past is not something that can be forgotten, or even that it should be.

Henry and I married yesterday. It was cold and the snow is up to our knees, but our hearts were warm. My only regret is that you were not there by my side.

It is too soon for any letters you have sent to have reached me, so I do not know the details of your circumstances. Just know: if you are happy in Chicago, then I am happy for you. If you want to return to Montana Territory, you will always have a home with me.

You are the daughter of my heart.

Love,

Bertha

ABOUT THE AUTHOR

Dana Alden lives in Bozeman, Montana with her husband and children. Dana has lived in Canada, Japan, and parts of the U.S., but her heart is in Montana. Dana writes the Mountain Men of Montana Series and the Darlington Family Saga Series.

Stay in touch! If you'd like to know when Dana's next book releases, please visit her website at www.DanaAlden.com and join her mailing list.